Deadly
Stranger

Deadly Stranger

Peg Kehret

Dodd, Mead & Company
New York

Copyright © 1987 by Peg Kehret
Distributed in Canada by
McClelland and Stewart Limited, Toronto
Manufactured in the United States of America

1 2 3 4 5 6 7 8 9 10

Library of Congress Cataloging-in-Publication Data

Kehret, Peg.
Deadly stranger.

Summary: When twelve-year-old Shannon is kidnapped by
a psychopath, her new friend, Katie, finds her life in
danger when she unknowingly becomes the kidnapper's
only witness.
[1. Kidnapping—Fiction. 2. Mentally ill—Fiction]
I. Title.
PZ7.K2518De 1987   [Fic]   86-32873
ISBN 0-396-09039-7

For Anne Konen

My daughter, my (true) friend

Deadly Stranger

1

Katie Osborne hoped she wouldn't throw up.

As she walked toward Franklin Middle School on her first day as a student there, she thought there was a distinct possibility that she would lose her breakfast. What if no one talked to her? What if her hair was all wrong?

Katie's brown hair was short and curly, the way most of the girls back in Mill Valley wore their hair. But the fashion here in Franklin might be different. Maybe all the girls would have long, straight hair.

She shouldn't have had another perm. She should just have curled it with a curling iron. That way, she could wash all the curl out if everybody else had straight hair.

She wished she'd never left Mill Valley. If she were walking toward her old school, she'd know what to expect. And she wouldn't be walking alone; she'd be walking with Bitsy, her best friend in the whole world whom she had known since she was three years old.

What if she was the only girl who had on a dress instead of pants? Worst of all, what if she was the tallest person in the entire seventh grade? She'd throw up for sure, if that happened.

All through sixth grade, she'd been the tallest. Even though she scrunched down whenever possible, she was always put in the back row for class pictures, and if there weren't enough boys to go around when they did square dancing in P.E., the teacher asked Katie to dance the boy's part. She hated it.

She drank coffee whenever she got the chance, which wasn't often. She hoped it would stunt her growth, but so far it hadn't worked. Maybe she didn't drink enough of it to do any good.

Her sister, Linda, liked being tall. "You'll like it, too, when you're older," Linda said. "Tall women wear their clothes well. That's why most fashion models are tall."

It was easy for Linda to say. She was out of school and married and expecting her second baby in six weeks. Nobody made *her* dance the boy's part in P.E.

Linda was the main reason Katie's family had moved. She and her husband, Mark, and their little boy, Sammy, lived in Franklin. When Katie's father was offered a transfer, it meant they could all live in the same town again for the first time since Linda and Mark got married.

Katie had to admit it was fun to see Linda, Mark, and Sammy more often. Mark taught her to play chess and now they had a tournament going. And Linda, who liked to sew, had offered to make Katie some new clothes. Still, she wasn't sure it was worth leaving Mill Valley and all her friends for. She was quite positive it wasn't worth starting in a new school for.

It didn't even look like a school. Her school in Mill Valley was a big, stone building, three stories tall with ivy growing up the sides. The Franklin school was a series of one-story structures, built in a U-shape around a central courtyard. It looked like a motel, not a school.

Katie took a deep breath, swallowed twice, and crossed the parking lot toward the main entrance. All the kids were talking and laughing. Everybody seemed to know everybody else. Everybody but her. Her stomach threatened to erupt but she swallowed again and headed for the office.

She knew where it was because her mother had brought her to register yesterday, after school was out for the day. Today she had to pick up her schedule of classes.

Her first class was American History. Fortunately, it

was just down the hall from the office so Katie had no trouble finding it. She gave the teacher, Mr. Gates, her pink New Student Registration Slip and he gave her a textbook. Then she found an empty desk and sat down, trying to watch the other kids arrive without staring at them.

She was relieved to see that several of the girls who came in wore dresses and had short, curly hair. At least she didn't look like a freak. Some of the kids seemed at least as tall as she was, too. Maybe taller. It was hard to tell for sure when she was sitting down and they were standing, but she was almost positive that she was not the tallest person in American History. Katie relaxed a little.

A girl with reddish-blonde hair took the seat next to Katie. She smiled as she sat down and Katie smiled back.

"Hi," the girl said. "I'm Shannon Lindstrom."

"I'm Katie Osborne."

"Are you new?"

Katie nodded. "This is my first day."

Shannon wrinkled up her nose and rolled her eyes. "Poor you," she said. "I've moved three times so I know what it's like. It's gross."

"It's more than gross," Katie agreed. "It's Saint Bernard gross."

"Who's he?"

Katie hesitated. She hadn't meant to say that; it just

12

slipped out. But now that she'd said it, she supposed she had to explain.

"I'm planning to be a veterinarian someday," she said. "My specialty is going to be dogs, so sometimes I think in terms of dogs, just to get in the habit of it. When I said starting a new school was Saint Bernard gross, I meant it's *hugely* gross. A big problem."

Shannon giggled. "I like that," she said. "I've had a few Saint Bernard gross problems myself." She cocked her head to one side and studied Katie. "You'll have to take a lot of science and math if you're going to be a veterinarian," she said.

"I don't care. I *like* science and math."

"So do I," Shannon said. "I want to be a psychiatrist and study disturbed people."

"You could start with my little brother," Katie said. "Pooch is a purebred, registered crazy person."

"His name is Pooch? That's pretty funny, since you plan to specialize in dogs."

"His name is William but he has these big, soulful brown eyes, like a cocker spaniel, and when he was a baby my dad started calling him Pooch. The name stuck." She grinned at Shannon. "We also have a dog," she said. "His name's Fred."

They were still laughing at that when Mr. Gates rapped his ruler on the desk and asked the class to turn to page 97 in their books.

"You'll like Mr. Gates," Shannon whispered. "He's my favorite teacher."

When American History ended, Shannon said, "What's your next class?"

Katie consulted her schedule. "English. Room 38."

"I'll walk with you," Shannon said. "My next class is in Room 36."

As they walked, Shannon asked Katie about her family.

"My dad's an electrical engineer," Katie said. "Mom's a nurse but she's taking a few months off to fix up our new house and get everyone settled. Pooch is in third grade and he's a pain in the neck. My sister and her husband and their little boy live in Franklin, too."

"You're already an aunt?" Shannon said. "That's neat! Your folks waited long enough between having your sister and having you, didn't they?"

"Twelve years."

"My family's spread out, too," Shannon said. "There's ten years between my brother and me."

"Then maybe you'll be an aunt before long, too."

Shannon shook her head. "No way," she said.

They arrived at Room 38 before Katie could learn more about Shannon but they made arrangements to meet again at lunchtime in the cafeteria. Katie felt a lot better about being new, now that she had someone to sit with at lunch. At least she wouldn't be left all alone at a table, like she had chicken pox, or something.

Shannon introduced Katie to two other girls who sat at their table in the cafeteria. Brooke was short and pudgy and giggled a lot—a Pomeranian, Katie decided. Pam was lanky, with sleek, black hair and a sophisticated style. Definitely a Doberman.

They were discussing an awards dinner which was scheduled that night for the girls' basketball team.

"I think Pam will get Player of the Year," Brooke said.

"Me? No way," Pam said. "Ginger Edgeworth will get that for sure."

"You scored as many points as she did," Brooke said.

"But she's Coach Robert's pet," Pam said. "She stays late every day to help clean up the gym."

"That's true," Brooke said. "Maybe you should have stayed late sometimes and helped clean up."

"I can't," Pam said. "If I miss the Activities Bus, I don't have any way to get home."

"Well, *I* don't think Coach Robert will judge on anything but how you played in the games," Shannon said. "The award isn't given for neatness."

"Then Pam will win," Brooke said. "Remember those two free throws she made in the final three seconds in the game against Kenmore? Ginger never did anything like that."

Katie listened, feeling out of it. It was hard to care who won Player of the Year when she didn't know any of the players and hadn't seen any of the games. She

15

missed Bitsy. Last year, she and Bitsy went to all the Mill Valley girls' basketball games together and cheered and yelled 'till their throats hurt.

As she walked out of the cafeteria with Brooke, Pam, and Shannon, Katie still felt lonely. She'd move back to Mill Valley in a minute, if she could. She sighed. Since she couldn't, at least it helped to know that all the kids here weren't nerds. Pam and Brooke seemed OK—and she liked Shannon a lot. If she could make friends with someone like Shannon, she might just survive.

The next morning, as Katie headed toward school for her second day, she wasn't so nervous. Yesterday she'd dreaded walking into the school. Now she knew it wasn't a complete horror, so she only minded a little. She pushed open the door, started toward her locker, and stopped.

Something was wrong. It was too quiet in the school. Katie looked around, wondering what was the matter. Some of the girls were crying and even the boys, who had been so rowdy yesterday, now had sad, hound-dog looks. Groups of students clustered close together in the hall, talking in hushed tones.

Katie hesitated. She wanted to ask what was wrong but she felt shy. She looked around for a familiar face, maybe one of the girls she'd met at lunch yesterday, Brooke or Pam. She saw no one she recognized, so she

continued down the hall to American History. Perhaps Shannon would know what was going on.

Shannon wasn't there yet. Katie got out her history book and removed the note she'd written to Shannon last night. As soon as Shannon arrived, Katie planned to hand her the note.

Shannon still wasn't there when the bell rang. Mr. Gates walked to the front of the room and everyone quieted immediately. He didn't even have to rap on his desk with his ruler.

"I know that some of you have already heard the news," Mr. Gates said. "For those who have not, I'm sorry to tell you that one of your classmates, Shannon Lindstrom, has been missing since yesterday. There is no reason to think that Shannon ran away from home but if she did, and if you know where she might be, you will be doing her a big favor if you tell the police or her parents."

Katie stared at Mr. Gates. Shannon was missing? How could she be missing when Katie had just seen her yesterday?

"At times like this," Mr. Gates continued, "there are always a lot of rumors which aren't true and which serve no useful purpose. I've just come from a faculty meeting with Detective Collins from the Franklin Police, so my information is accurate. If any of you has heard any story about what happened to Shannon, I'd like

you to say so now, so that we all get the facts straight."

He paused and looked expectantly around the room.

A boy in the back raised his hand.

"Yes, Justin?"

"I heard that Shannon was murdered and they found her body at the bottom of Lake Duvall."

Katie felt a hollowness inside. Even though it was warm in the room and she was still wearing her blue cardigan sweater, she shivered.

"That isn't true," Mr. Gates said. "Shannon has not been found. She is still missing. That's why it's so important for anyone who knows anything at all about where she might be, to come forward."

Katie saw several of the kids look at each other in relief. Apparently, they'd heard the same story Justin had heard, about Shannon being murdered. No wonder some of the girls had been crying. It was bad enough for Shannon to be missing; it was unthinkable for her to be dead. She was only twelve years old, the same as Katie. People twelve years old aren't supposed to die. Not for a long, long time.

A girl by the window spoke next. "I heard that Shannon's parents are divorced and the one who didn't get to keep her came and took her away," she said.

Only a week or two earlier, Katie had watched a movie on TV about that very thing, so it sounded logical.

Mr. Gates shook his head. "Shannon's parents are not

divorced," he said. "They live together and they are both extremely upset and worried over Shannon's disappearance."

A few other kids ventured guesses about what might have happened but it was clear that none of them really knew. All anybody knew for sure was that Shannon was gone and neither the police nor her parents nor Mr. Gates had any idea where she was.

"They've found no evidence of foul play," Mr. Gates said. "No one broke into the Lindstrom home and no one in the neighborhood remembers seeing anything unusual. That's why the police think she may have run away and that's why it's crucial that if any of you know where she is, for you to say so."

The room was silent.

"All right," Mr. Gates said. "Since none of you has any information about Shannon, we'll continue our study of the Civil War. Please open your books to page 106."

Katie looked down at her book. Lying on top of it was the note she'd written last night. She opened the paper slowly and stared at her own handwriting.

Mon. 10 P.M.

Dear Shannon:

Did your brother tell you I was there? I came to say I couldn't go shopping because I had to baby-sit with Pooch but it didn't matter because you were at your piano lesson anyway. If you want to go shopping today instead, I can go with you. Let me know after class.

I was scared of starting a new school until I met you. I thought I'd do something stupid like getting lost between classes or not being able to find the bathroom. I should have known that future veterinarians and psychiatrists don't do stupid things.

Your new (true) friend,
Katie

P.S. I'd write more but I'm DOG tired.

Carefully, Katie refolded the note and put it back inside her history book. She wondered when Shannon would get to read it.

Or if.

2

Katie didn't listen to Mr. Gates. The Civil War no longer seemed important, not when Shannon was missing.

Mentally, Katie reviewed everything that had happened after school the day before, starting with the discovery that she and Shannon lived less than six blocks from each other.

"No kidding!" Shannon had said, when Katie told her the address. "We can walk partway home together."

Katie quickly got her coat from her locker, which was just down the hall from Shannon's locker. She noticed that most of the kids had posters on the insides of their locker doors. She would have to bring a poster for her locker, too. Maybe she would bring the one she got from

The Humane Society. GET THE BEST OF EVERY-THING, it said. The picture was of a funny-looking mutt with his various body parts labeled: the ears of a German shepherd, the feet of a giant schnauzer, the tail of a boxer. Katie laughed every time she looked at the poster.

"I need to go to the shopping center this afternoon and get some more notebooks," Shannon said. "Do you want to come with me?"

"Sure," Katie said. "But I have to go home first and let my mom know where I'm going."

As they walked home, Shannon said, "It's nice to finally meet somebody who likes science and math. Half the girls I know won't talk about anything except boys."

"I know the feeling," Katie said. All last summer, Bitsy drove her crazy, raving on about how cute Gordon McDowell was. Personally, Katie thought Gordon McDowell resembled a greyhound. His legs were too long and skinny for the rest of him and he had a pointed nose. All he lacked was the tail. She never told Bitsy that, though. Bitsy thought Gordon was a real hunk.

"Not that I have anything against guys," Shannon went on. "But a boyfriend isn't the most important thing in the universe."

"I know a few girls who would disagree."

"Even my parents expect me to like what all the other girls like," Shannon said. "Sometimes I feel like a freak because I don't think the way I'm supposed to think."

"You don't sound freaky to me."

"Maybe not a freak, exactly, but different. When I was still in grade school, I always wanted a chemistry set or a telescope for my birthday."

"I got a microscope when I was ten," Katie said, "and it's the best birthday present I ever got."

"Not me," said Shannon. "I always got stupid Barbie dolls and crummy little perfume sets. I never got what I really wanted."

Katie nodded sympathetically. "The worst present I ever got was a pair of pantyhose," she said. "I was eight and my grandma thought I'd be thrilled with what she called a 'grown-up' gift. I wasn't thrilled; I was disgusted. What did I want with pantyhose when I had plenty of perfectly good ankle socks?"

"Your folks seem willing to let you grow up," Shannon said. "Mine want me to always be their baby girl."

They reached the corner where Shannon had to turn. She told Katie how to find her house. "Look for the pots of white geraniums on the steps."

"I'll be there as fast as I can. And thanks for asking me. I needed a friend today."

Shannon grinned. "New friend, true friend," she said.

"See you soon," Katie said as she crossed the street and continued on her way. When she approached the red brick rambler that was now the Osborne home, she noticed her mom's car wasn't in the driveway. She got out her key and went inside but only Fred was there to greet her, thumping his tail on the floor and giving excited little yips. Katie scratched his ears and let him out into the backyard.

There was a note on the kitchen table.

Katie: Linda's car broke down and I have to drive her to her doctor's appointment. Please keep an eye on Pooch. I'll be home about 5:30. Love, Mom.

"Rats," Katie muttered to herself. Wouldn't you know? The first time Shannon asked her to do something, she couldn't go because she was stuck at home with her little brother. Pooch's school started an hour later than Katie's and got out a half hour later. He'd be home any minute.

She let Fred back in and gave him his dog biscuit. It was a ritual with Fred. It began when he was a puppy and was being house-trained. Whenever he went outside to do his business, he was rewarded with a dog biscuit as soon as he came back in.

Fred caught on quickly, and heaven help you now if you let him back in and neglected to give him the biscuit. Fred would follow after you and whine relentlessly until you remembered. Sometimes the Osbornes suspected that Fred went out solely for the purpose of coming back in and collecting his reward.

Fred was smart; there was no doubt about that. Katie

kept a vocabulary list of words that Fred understood and it was now up to twenty-six different words. And that didn't include the sound of the can opener, which Fred could also identify.

While Fred ate his biscuit, Katie poured herself a glass of milk and munched on some peanut butter cookies. She also looked through the mail to see if there were any letters for her but there weren't. When she moved, Bitsy and some of the other kids in Mill Valley had promised they'd write ("Every day," Bitsy said. "Without fail!") but so far nobody had. Bitsy was probably too busy looking gaga at Gordon the Greyhound; that's why she didn't write.

"Mom! Mom! Guess what!" Pooch came charging in the door, the way he always did, shouting at the top of his lungs and dropping his sweater in a heap on the floor.

"Mom isn't home," Katie said. "She took Linda to the doctor."

"Guess what happened at school," Pooch said.

Now how was she supposed to guess? "The teacher dyed her hair green," Katie said, "and sang hard rock songs to the class."

Pooch giggled. "No, silly," he said. "We all had to write a paper on what we did during summer vacation and the most interesting ones got displayed in the hall and mine's one of them."

"What did you write about?"

"My dog show."

"That would be an interesting paper, all right," Katie said. Pooch's dog show, like most of Pooch's money-making ideas, had been a disaster. He spent days putting up posters about it and making ribbons to be awarded as prizes.

On the day of the show, it rained, so instead of having it in the yard, he had it in the Osbornes' garage. Even though Pooch charged a 50¢ entry fee, fourteen kids showed up with their dogs, two of which hated each other on sight. They began growling and snapping and that alarmed some of the other dogs and *they* started barking and before long there was a huge ruckus.

Three dogs bolted away from their owners and one of them knocked over two bags of aluminum cans that were waiting to go to the recycling center. The clatter of the cans panicked the rest of the dogs and there was a mad scramble for the door. A big ladder got knocked over and one kid got his foot tangled in a leash and fell down and broke his elbow. Mrs. Osborne called the medic emergency number and an ambulance came and all the neighbors came running over to see what had happened and the ribbons for Biggest Dog, Smallest Dog, Most Unusual-looking Dog, and Best of Show never did get awarded. Mr. and Mrs. Osborne made Pooch return all the entry fees.

Yes, Katie could see why an account of Pooch's dog show would be interesting enough to be displayed in the hall.

She got out the telephone directory and looked under the *L*s for Lindstrom. One of them was on the street where Shannon lived so Katie dialed the number. No one answered. That was odd. Shannon said her home was only three blocks from where Katie turned; surely she was home by now. Maybe she was waiting outside for Katie to come and didn't hear the phone.

"We have to go for a walk," Katie told Pooch. "I met a girl at school and she's expecting me to come over and I have to let her know I'm not coming."

"That's dumb," Pooch said. "How can you go over there to tell her you aren't going over there?"

"I have to tell her I'm not going shopping with her."

"Why not?"

"Because Mom wants me to stay with you."

Pooch looked indignant. "I don't need you to baby-sit with me," he said. "I can take care of myself."

That was debatable. Pooch was forever getting into some kind of mess and Katie knew he shouldn't be left home alone. But she also remembered how she'd hated having a sitter a couple of years ago, when she thought *she* was big enough to stay alone.

"I know you can," she said. "But you know how Mom worries about us. We just have to humor her."

Pooch nodded and helped himself to the cookies.

"It isn't far," Katie said. "All we have to do is walk over to her house, tell her I'm not going shopping with her, and come back home."

"OK," Pooch said. He stuffed six more cookies in his pants' pockets, three on each side. "In case I get hungry on the way," he said.

They walked together for the first block but then Pooch got interested in the way the water ran down the gutters and Katie got farther and farther ahead. By the time she got to Shannon's street, Pooch was a full two blocks behind her. She could still see him so she decided to let him dawdle. She'd catch up to him again on the way home.

She recognized Shannon's house immediately from the description Shannon had given her—brown shingles, two-story, with pots of white geraniums on the front steps.

Katie walked up the steps and rang the doorbell. There was no answer. She waited a minute and then knocked. Had she misunderstood? No, she was sure Shannon had asked her to come today.

As she turned to leave, she thought she heard something, but the sound was so muffled she couldn't be certain. She waited, listening, but she heard nothing more.

She stepped away from the house and looked down the street. Pooch was still on the curb, poking a stick at something in the gutter. Katie wondered if Shannon might be in the backyard, where she couldn't hear the doorbell. Maybe the Lindstroms had a dog, too, and Shannon was playing with it.

She followed the cement path around the side of the house, past some shrubs and a clothesline, the collapsible kind that fits into a hole in the ground. She saw no one in the backyard.

"Shannon?" Katie called. "Are you here?"

Ordinarily, she would not have been so persistent. Usually, if she went to someone's house and nobody answered the doorbell, Katie would turn around and leave. But Shannon had asked her to come, less than an hour ago. It seemed strange that she wouldn't wait for Katie to get there. She didn't seem like the kind of girl who would invite someone to come over and then just up and leave without even calling.

Of course, she didn't know Katie's phone number or even her address and the Osbornes weren't listed in the directory yet. Maybe she couldn't even remember Katie's last name or how to spell it. Lots of people put a z where the s was supposed to be.

She returned to the front of the house, checked on Pooch, and climbed the porch steps again. She rang the doorbell one last time. There was a window to the right of the door and a slight movement caught her eye.

"Shannon?" she called. "It's me, Katie."

She leaned closer to the window and peered inside the house.

A young man stood in the living room. For a second he stared back at Katie. His look was hostile, as if he were angry that she was looking at him.

Katie quickly stepped away, embarrassed at being caught peeking in someone else's window. She hadn't meant to spy; she just wondered why Shannon didn't answer the door.

Even as she stepped back, the young man opened the door a crack. He was about twenty-two or twenty-three, with thick reddish hair. A golden retriever, Katie thought. She realized he must be Shannon's brother. Shannon had said there was ten years between them.

"Is Shannon here?" Katie said.

"No."

"She asked me to come over," Katie said. "Do you know where she is?"

"Piano lesson." He mumbled in such a low voice that Katie could barely make out what he said.

"Would you please tell her I was here?" Katie said. "And give this to her?" She fished in her purse for a pencil and piece of paper and quickly jotted her name and phone number on it. She added her address, too, just in case Shannon wanted it.

She handed the paper to Shannon's brother.

"Thanks," she said.

He took the paper and closed the door. He certainly wasn't as friendly as Shannon. Still, Katie felt better as she started back down the street toward Pooch. Shannon's absence made sense now. She probably forgot about her piano lesson and then, when she remembered, she didn't know how to call Katie to tell her not to come over.

She wondered why Shannon's brother didn't answer the door right away. If Katie hadn't looked through the window and seen him inside, he might not have opened it at all. Brothers! It was exactly the sort of thing Pooch would do—ignore a knock on the door because he was busy building a model or figuring out a new plan to make money.

Pooch always had some scheme that was going to make him a lot of money. Most of them ended up like his dog show—a disaster.

She would tell Shannon tomorrow that her brother looked like a golden retriever. Make that a golden retriever who's been in a dog fight. That would account for the scar on his forehead.

Pooch was still fooling around in the gutter, making little boats out of leaves and twigs and letting them float down to the corner, where they piled up like a log jam on top of the sewer drain.

"I'm going to put on a boat race," he announced.

"Let's go home," Katie said.

For once, he didn't argue, probably because he'd eaten all his cookies and wanted to get some more.

Katie intended to call Shannon that night and ask how the piano lesson went but she didn't get a chance because Linda, Mark, and Sammy were there for dinner. Linda was having a hard time with this pregnancy and was supposed to rest a lot which wasn't easy to do with Sammy getting into everything.

By the time they left and she thought about Shannon, it was too late to call.

After she got ready for bed, she got out her notebook and pencil and sat in bed with her knees propped up. She had planned to write a letter to Bitsy, to tell her about the new school, but she was disgusted with Bitsy for not writing back. She decided to write a note to Shannon instead.

It was fun to get notes in school, even if it did take longer to write something than to say it. She wanted to tell Shannon how worried she'd been about starting a new school and how it had turned out OK.

As she sat quietly, planning what to say, light from a pair of headlights shone through her window and moved across the wall. Whenever a car turned the corner from 29th Avenue to Hickory Street, the lights shone briefly into Katie's window. This time, though, the lights stopped, backed up, and then went forward again, slowly.

Curious, Katie got out of bed and went to the window. There was a green car in front of her house and whoever was in it was shining a flashlight at the front door, as if to read the house numbers. Odd. They wouldn't be getting company at this time of the night. She could tell the car was green but the streetlight was too faint for her to see the driver.

Katie put her face against the window and cupped her hands beside her eyes, to get a better look. Almost immediately, the flashlight went off and the car drove away.

Katie shivered in her pajamas, scurried back to her warm bed, and began to write.

Mon. 10 P.M.

Dear Shannon:

Did your brother tell you I was there?

The bell rang, ending American History for the day and jangling Katie out of her memory of last night and back to the present. Last night, she thought she was writing the first of many such notes to her new friend.

Now she wondered if this note was not only the first but also the last.

"Remember," Mr. Gates said, as they all stood up to leave, "if anyone knows where Shannon Lindstrom is, tell me—or tell the police."

3

After she left Katie at the corner, Shannon hurried home. She wanted to change into her jeans before Katie got there. No point walking to the shopping center in a skirt if she could be comfortable instead.

She was going to like this new girl, she could tell. It was about time she met someone like herself who was interested in something besides eye makeup and boys. She was glad Katie wanted to go shopping with her. It would give them some time to talk and find out what else they had in common.

She let herself in as usual, went straight to the kitchen for an apple, and was just going to take her first bite when a voice behind her said, "Hello, Angie." Shannon jumped and whirled around to see who was there.

He stood in the dining room, watching her.

She screamed, as loudly as she could, but it didn't do any good. No one heard her. As soon as she screamed, the man rushed into the kitchen, grabbed her, pushed her hard against the refrigerator, and stuffed a dish towel in her mouth. Then he used an apron to tie her hands behind her back.

"Shut up," he said. "Shut up or they'll come and get us and lock us up again."

Shannon stared at him, her heart pounding in her throat. What did he mean, they would lock us up again? Was he an escaped prisoner?

He was tall, six-feet-one at least, maybe six-two, and he was lean and muscular. He might have been good looking, except for the jagged scar on his forehead. And his eyes. His eyes were strange, animal-like, and when he looked at her, it seemed that he didn't quite focus.

Shannon wondered how he got in. The door was locked, as it always was, when she came home.

The telephone rang. Shannon jumped. She hoped the man would answer it. Sometimes Shannon's mother called her from work about this time, just to say *hi* and to see how Shannon's day went. If a man answered the phone, Mom would know something was wrong.

He didn't move. He just looked at the phone, listening to it ring and ring, as if wondering what to do.

Answer it, Shannon thought. *Pick it up and say hello.*

The phone quit ringing. If it was her mother, Shannon knew she'd call again in a few minutes, unless her office got too busy.

When the phone quit ringing, he nodded at one of the kitchen chairs. "Sit down, Angie," he said.

Shannon sat. She didn't know what else to do. Why did he keep calling her Angie? She didn't know anyone named Angie.

She watched as the man wandered around the kitchen, opening drawers and closing them again, looking in the cupboards. He opened the drawer where the Lindstroms kept their good silverware, the set Shannon's mom inherited from her grandmother. The man glanced at it and closed the drawer. What did he want? What was he looking for? Any burglar in his right mind would grab that sterling silver.

In his right mind. Maybe this man wasn't in his right mind. Maybe he was totally crazy. Shannon had done some reading about insane people and she knew they often did illogical things for no apparent reason. Some of them even did violent things. The thought was no comfort.

He was looking in the drawer by the kitchen sink when the doorbell rang. The man froze. So did Shannon.

She watched him. He didn't move. A few seconds later, whoever was at the door, knocked. Shannon knew she had to do something. She couldn't let whoever was there leave without being aware of her problem.

She leaped to her feet and kicked at her chair, knocking it to the floor with a *thunk*. Instantly, the man was at her side, his arm around her neck, jerking her head backwards. In his other hand, he held the long, sharp knife that Shannon's mother used to chop vegetables.

He didn't say a word. He didn't have to. He simply held the knife where she could see it and she knew better than to make any more noise.

They waited. Shannon didn't hear the footsteps retreat from the front door or walk along the path beside the house. She heard nothing until a voice, unbelievably close, called out, "Shannon? Are you here?"

Shannon tensed. The man's grip tightened.

It was Katie, her new friend. *I'm in here,* Shannon wanted to shout. *Go for help, Katie! Call the police!*

It was quiet again and Shannon was sure Katie had gone home.

"Don't move," the man whispered in her ear. He must have thought Katie was gone, too, because he walked away from Shannon, through the dining room, into the living room. Just then, the doorbell rang again.

Shannon heard him answer, heard him tell Katie something about a piano. She wanted to run for the door, let Katie see her with the gag in her mouth, but she thought about the knife. The man still had the knife in his hand. What if he panicked? He might kill both of them. Even if Katie got away and ran for help, it wouldn't do much good for the police to come and find Shannon stabbed to death. She remained where she was.

As the door closed, tears ran slowly down her cheeks.

The man waited a few minutes. Then, after looking cautiously out the window several times, he took her by the arm and led her out the back door, pushing the automatic lock before he closed the door behind them. He took her past the detached garage, to the seldom-used alley which ran between the Lindstroms' backyard and that of their neighbors to the rear.

His car was parked there, an old sedan with peeling green paint. He opened the back door of the car and motioned for Shannon to get in. Then he made her lie down on the floor and he put a faded blanket over her. It was hot under the blanket and hard to breathe.

As he started the engine, he said, "Lie still, Angie. After we get away from here, you can get up."

At first, Shannon tried to figure out which way they were going. She knew the car turned to the right when it left the alley and a short time later, it turned right again. That would put them on 28th Avenue. Three turns later, she gave up trying to keep track. The man appeared to be aimlessly going in circles. Sometimes it felt like they were speeding and other times it seemed they were going slow. She hoped he might need to stop for gas. If he pulled into a service station, Shannon planned to sit up and try to attract attention fast.

He didn't stop. He kept driving and eventually Shannon could hear no other traffic sounds and she realized they must be out in the country.

The car bumped along, as if the road they were on was not paved. With her hands tied behind her back, Shannon couldn't brace herself well and her head kept bouncing on the floor.

By the time he finally stopped, she felt like she'd been put through a food processor.

"You can get out," he said.

She stepped from the car into weeds that came almost to her knees. An old barn, with its door hanging loosely from one hinge, was just ahead. Shannon looked quickly in all directions, hoping to bolt to freedom, but she saw no other buildings. There were no lights, no sign of any human activity, not even a road in the distance. All she saw was barren land and a tree or two.

It was getting dark and the old barn with its weathered boards and sloping roof had a sinister look. The man took her by the arm and led her inside.

There was no evidence that he had been here before. There was no bedding, no sign of food. It was just an abandoned barn, somewhere in an empty field.

She wondered if this had been his destination all along or if he had just happened across it. Most of all, she wondered what he planned to do now that they were here.

Her jaw ached and her mouth was incredibly dry. "Mmmmpff," she said, and rolled her neck around. "Mmmmppff!"

He looked at her. "OK," he said. "Nobody can hear you now, anyway."

He removed the gag from Shannon's mouth.

"What about my hands?" she said, but he shook his head.

"I have to go to the bathroom."

He hesitated. "OK," he said. "I'll untie you long enough for that. But don't try to run away because you'd never make it."

She knew he was right about that. He'd be able to overtake her easily.

Was it her imagination or had he sounded more normal just now? It was hard to tell for sure, but his eyes didn't seem quite as wild as they had earlier. Maybe he'd been on some kind of drug and was hallucinating. That would explain why he kept calling her Angie. Maybe now it was wearing off and he would come to his senses and take her back.

As soon as she finished in the weeds, he tied her hands

again and made her lie on the floor of the barn, up against one wall. He sat near the doorway, smoking and looking out at the darkening sky.

Shannon thought about her parents. Her mom would be home from work by now and would discover that Shannon was gone. She wouldn't wait long to report it; Shannon was sure of that. She had strict instructions to always leave a note if she wasn't going to be home when Mom got there and she always did it. Always.

So by now they knew she was missing. By now her parents would have called the police and a search would be underway for her. She wondered how soon the story would be broadcast on the radio and television. When would Katie hear it?

That was her best chance of being found quickly. As soon as Katie heard that Shannon was missing, she would tell the police about the man who had been in Shannon's house. She would be able to describe him and the police had artists who could make a composite drawing from the description and then the newspapers would print the drawing.

He was not ordinary looking, with his reddish hair and his scar. Those were distinctive features, the kinds of things people notice and remember. Surely someone would recognize him, maybe even know what kind of car to look for.

The trouble was, even when they knew who they were

looking for, nobody would know where to look.

"We should have been together," the man said. "It wasn't right. I wanted to find you but they wouldn't let me. Every time I tried to go back to you, they wouldn't let me."

"I'm not who you think I am," Shannon said. "You have the wrong person."

He acted as if he didn't hear her. "They shouldn't have locked me up," he said. "They should have let me find you."

There it was again—locked him up. He must be an escaped convict. She wondered what crime he had committed. Probably not robbery. He didn't steal her great-grandmother's sterling silver and surely an experienced thief would have taken that. She started to think of other possible crimes and then made herself stop. They were all too horrible to consider.

His voice had a faraway, dreamy quality. "We'll make a fresh start now," he said. "Just you and me, Angie. Maybe we'll get us a little farm somewhere, a piece of land all our own, far away from all of them."

"Can't you hear what I'm telling you?" Shannon said. "I'M NOT ANGIE!" She had to convince him of that. Once he realized he had the wrong person, maybe he would let her go. But how was she going to convince him when he wouldn't listen?

She wished she'd been able to bring her purse along.

She had her school pictures in her purse and the student identification card that she had to present when she bought tickets for the football and basketball games. If she could show him those, then he'd believe her.

But her purse was home, on the kitchen table, where she'd put it when she got home from school.

Then she remembered something. The cafeteria card! She still had her cafeteria card in her pocket. She'd stuffed it in her pocket when she bought lunch, intending to put it back in her purse when she sat down at the table, only she got to talking with Katie and had never put her card away.

"I want to show you something," she said.

The man looked at her.

"It's in my pocket," she said. "You can get it out yourself, if you want to. You don't even have to untie me."

He got up and walked over to her. He stood, looking down at her. "What is it?" he said.

"It's my cafeteria card. From school. You have to buy a new card every month and then they punch the date when you get your lunch. Mine's in my right-hand pocket of my sweater and it has my name on it. Look at it, if you don't believe me. It says I'm Shannon Lindstrom, not Angie somebody."

She waited, looking up at him. Why didn't he get the

card out and look at it? What was he waiting for?

"The card is in my pocket," she said again. "I want you to look at it."

He knelt beside her and put his hand in her pocket. She didn't like having him so close but she tried not to recoil. He removed the card, stood up again, and looked at it.

"Do you see?" she said. "Right there at the top, it has my name. It says *Shannon Lindstrom. Grade 7.*"

He stared at the card.

"Do you see it?"

"Yes," he said. He dropped the card on the floor of the barn and returned to where he had been sitting.

"Well?" she said. "Do you believe me now?"

"They told me you were dead," he said. "They wouldn't let me hunt for you. They said you died in the accident, too, the same as Mother, but I knew they were lying. They locked me up so I couldn't find you but I knew they were lying."

Tears of anger and frustration brimmed in Shannon's eyes. Why wouldn't he listen to her? Hadn't he heard a thing she'd just told him?

"I am not Angie," she said. "My name is Shannon Lindstrom."

"I knew I'd find you, if I had the chance," he said. "I knew you'd still be there, waiting for me to come home and I was right. And now they don't know where we are and they'll never find us. We can stay together always and they'll never find us. Never!"

"Oh, yes, they will," Shannon cried. "By now my parents have called the police and they'll be looking for me. And my friend, Katie, saw you. She saw you when you answered the door. Katie got a good, long look at you and she'll tell the police what you look like and they'll find us!"

He heard her that time. He jumped up, strode toward her and stood over her, glaring down. His face was shadowy in the darkness of the barn but she could feel his anger. She could hear his hard, fast breathing and could sense the tenseness of his body.

"No!" he said. "They won't find us. I'll never go back."

"But you've made a terrible mistake. I'm not who you think I am. The police are already looking for us; I know they are."

He kicked her, hard, his heavy boot catching her on the hipbone. Shannon cried out from the sudden pain.

"Shut up!" he yelled.

She lay still, trying not to cry. Her hipbone throbbed but she would not utter another sound. Let him call her Angie. She wouldn't argue with him again. Let him think anything he wanted, as long as he stayed on the other side of the barn.

He turned away from her and began to pace. He

walked back and forth in the darkness, back and forth, like a caged panther Shannon had seen once in a zoo. She'd felt sorry for the panther. It shouldn't have been locked up like that; it should have been free to run in the jungle or wherever panthers lived.

She didn't feel sorry for this man. She hated him. He had no right to do this to her. To kidnap her and keep her tied up and kick her. Well, she would get away from him. She would wait until he went to sleep and then she'd run away. She could still run, even with her hands tied, and if he slept very long, she'd get enough of a start that he couldn't catch her before she found someone to help.

After awhile, the man quit pacing. He sat in the doorway of the barn again and smoked another cigarette. Shannon could see the tiny glow of light and smell the smoke.

It was getting hard to stay awake. Her head ached, partly from hunger, she thought, and partly from anxiety. Her whole body felt exhausted, as if she'd been up for days. She stared at the tip of the cigarette and her eyes burned with fatigue. She decided to close them, just for a few moments, just to rest them. She could still listen. She would know when the man finally went to sleep because she'd be able to hear his deep, steady breathing.

She closed her eyes and lay still in the darkness, listening to the silence. Gradually, her tense muscles relaxed. She took a deep breath and shifted to her right side, the way she always did in her bed at home every night, just before she went to sleep.

Stay awake, she told herself. You have to stay awake until he falls asleep. She forced her eyelids open once more but she could no longer see the cigarette. Maybe he was finally going to lie down and go to sleep.

She would listen for him. She would listen hard, but her eyelids were so heavy, so very heavy. She let them fall closed once more.

She woke suddenly, startled by the sound of a car's engine, approaching the barn. Her eyes flew open as the sound came closer and stopped. A car door slammed. Shannon's heart pounded. Someone must have spotted the man's car and come to investigate.

She sat up, looking around the barn. She couldn't be sure in the dim moonlight, but she thought the man was gone. She was alone.

"I'm in here!" she yelled, and she tried to get to her feet.

His tall frame filled the doorway. "I know where you are, Angie," he said.

Shannon stared at him. He held a large brown paper bag. He set it on the floor, turned on a flashlight, and removed a bag of potato chips. "Got us some food," he said.

Tears of frustration filled Shannon's eyes. He had left, while she slept. He'd taken the car and driven somewhere and she hadn't heard him leave. Her chance to run, to escape from him, had passed and she hadn't even been aware of it.

She slumped back to the floor.

Several minutes passed and she heard no more cars. No one followed him, which meant he hadn't been recognized when he bought the food. She wondered if Katie had gone to the police yet. Katie might not even know yet that Shannon had been kidnapped. Maybe nobody knew yet who to look for. What was it the man told Katie? Something about a piano. Maybe he pretended he was there to tune the Lindstroms' piano. As soon as her parents heard that, they'd know what had happened. They didn't even own a piano.

She dozed fitfully the rest of the night, unable to get comfortable and also afraid he might leave again. She didn't want to blow her chance to escape a second time.

Eventually, she awoke to daylight. Her body ached from being in the same position for so long. Her head itched, from the dirt and old rotting hay on the barn floor. She wanted to scratch her scalp, but she couldn't. Not with her hands still tied.

She looked at her captor, sitting near the hole in the wall where a window once was. He was seated on a stack of old boards, drinking a beer and eating potato chips.

49

Shannon's stomach churned. Beer and potato chips were not her idea of a yummy breakfast, but she'd had nothing to eat since lunch the day before and she was famished.

"Do I get breakfast?" she asked.

He came over and stood next to her, looking down at her. Shannon tensed, fearful that he might kick her again.

Instead, he said, "Good morning," in a soft, gentle tone.

"Good morning," she replied warily. What was he up to now?

He knelt beside her and untied her hands. "There's plenty for both of us," he said.

He didn't sound like the same person. She didn't understand it but she was grateful for the change.

She stretched and wished she could brush her teeth. Then she saw the irony of such a wish. Here she was, held captive, and she was worried about brushing her teeth.

Mom and Dad would laugh when she told them. Billy would run to get one of his toys or try to turn a somersault to get their attention, like he always did when everyone laughed at something he didn't understand. Mom said it was typical behavior for a two-year-old.

Shannon swallowed hard. Would she ever see her family again?

The man handed her a can of orange soda.

"Is there anything else to drink?" she asked.

"But orange soda's your favorite," he said. "I got it especially for you."

She looked at the can of soda. It was the flavor she liked least and far too sweet for breakfast but there didn't seem to be much choice. She opened the can and took a sip, swallowing as quickly as she could.

She refused the potato chips, knowing they would only make her more thirsty. She ate two doughnuts instead. She didn't want to get weak from hunger. She needed to be strong and alert, in case there was another chance to get away.

"What's your name?" she asked.

He looked at her. His eyes seemed glazed again; his face subtly different. He must be on some kind of drug; he must have taken more of it this morning.

"Now don't be playing games with me," he said. "You know who I am, all right."

She decided it was best not to talk to him. Whenever she tried, she just got into more trouble. She returned to the far side of the barn and sat down, leaning her back against the wall. Maybe if she was quiet, he'd forget to tie her hands again.

The morning seemed to last forever. She wondered how long he expected to stay there. How long did he think the two of them could go on, hiding in the barn?

She saw him look at his watch more than once. Why did he care what time it was? Did he expect something to happen? Was someone else coming? She wanted to question him but she was afraid she'd make him angry again.

It was early afternoon, as far as Shannon could tell, when he abruptly stood up. He went to the car and returned shortly with a length of rope.

"I got to tie you, Angie," he said. "Got business in town. But I'll come back tonight. Don't worry; I'll be back."

"What sort of business?" Shannon asked.

His face darkened. "I don't like to do it," he said, "but she might tell."

"Who? What are you talking about?"

"She might. The one in the brick house."

Shannon gave up questioning him. He didn't make any sense and she didn't know anyone who lived in a brick house. Probably it was some friend of Angie's, whoever she was.

He bound her wrists tightly with the rope and then he tied her feet, too, wrapping the rope around her ankles and securing it to one of the large posts which supported the barn roof. She would never be able to get loose.

She lay in the dirt and watched him walk out the

door. She heard the car start, heard the engine fade into the distance. She closed her eyes and prayed that this time someone would recognize him from Katie's description.

4

Katie ate little of her lunch. The cafeteria had tacos, one of her favorite lunches, but she had no appetite. She was too upset to be interested in food. She didn't even eat the chocolate cookie and normally she'd have eaten that first.

She sat with Brooke and Pam and they talked about what might have happened to Shannon. All of the first period teachers had made the same announcement about Shannon that Mr. Gates made.

"She must have been kidnapped," Pam said.

"But who would do it?" Brooke said. "For what reason?"

It seemed odd to sit there with Brooke and Pam and discuss Shannon's disappearance when only yesterday,

Shannon was the one who introduced her to Brooke and Pam. Katie felt unreal, as if what was happening was just a bad dream.

She tried to concentrate on her afternoon classes but it was useless. Midway through fifth period, she got permission to go get a drink of water. In the hall, she saw a police officer and the principal. They were taking everything out of Shannon's locker.

Hope surged in Katie's mind and she hurried toward them. "Have you found her?" she asked. "Is Shannon home?"

The principal frowned at her and shook his head.

"Not yet," the officer said.

Katie lingered, watching them. She wondered if they were looking for something special. She also wondered if she should tell the officer who she was. It had occurred to her earlier in the day that the police might possibly want to question her. When Shannon's brother told them that a new girl, someone he'd never seen or heard of before, had been there asking for Shannon on the day she disappeared, they might just want to know what she wanted. Maybe she should say something right now, tell them that she was at Shannon's house and spoke with Shannon's older brother.

The principal looked at her. "Shouldn't you be in class?" he said.

"I left to get a drink of water."

"Then you'd best get it and return to your class," he said.

"Yes, sir," Katie said and she walked briskly toward the water fountain. The last thing she wanted was to get in trouble with the principal on her second day of school, and she could tell he didn't want her to bother the police officer. She'd already asked one question and the officer was probably in a hurry. Besides, Shannon's brother had her name, address, and phone number. If the police wanted to know why she'd gone to the Lindstroms' house yesterday, they knew where to reach her.

When the last bell finally rang, Katie dumped her books in her locker, grabbed her coat, and headed for the door. All she wanted to do was go home, listen to the news on the radio, and tell Mom and Pooch what had happened.

It was clouding over and the feel of rain was in the air. Katie walked fast, wanting to get home before the storm began.

When she got to the corner where she'd left Shannon the day before, she paused and looked in that direction. Just yesterday, Shannon had said, "New friend, true friend," and started down the sidewalk toward home.

What had happened to her? Katie knew she'd reached home safely. Shannon's brother had told her that, indirectly. But where was she now?

Katie was quite certain Shannon did not run away. Shannon might not get along perfectly with her folks but she was no bubblehead. She wouldn't do something stupid, like run away.

Katie stood on the corner, looking toward Shannon's house, and for the first time in her life she was deeply afraid for someone's safety. A kidnapping was something you read about in the newspaper or heard about on TV. It didn't happen to someone you knew, someone you cared about. Except this time, it had.

All day Katie had held back the tears. Now they threatened to overflow. She blinked hard, rounded the corner, and started across the street toward her own house.

She never heard the car. She was well into the street, half-blind from her tears, when it seemed to roar out of nowhere. She jumped and turned but she wasn't fast enough. She caught just a glimpse of a green car hurtling toward her before it struck her from behind.

There was an excruciating pain in her left leg and her purse flew out of her hand. She fell forward, smashing into the pavement with her right shoulder. Her cheek raked across the street's surface, tearing the skin and collecting dirt and tiny pebbles.

The wind was knocked out of her and she lay completely still for a second, her eyes closed. The car that hit her roared away.

She knew she should try to get a license number. Even in her shock, she knew the driver should not be leaving. She tried to sit up but the pain was too great. Instead of seeing a license plate, she saw only blackness and, with a moan, she fell back onto the concrete.

When she came to, there was a blanket on her. Someone was wiping her face with a cool, damp cloth. She could hear a siren in the distance, wailing, coming closer. She tried to open her eyes but the effort was more than she could manage. Through the haze of her pain, she heard her mother's voice.

"It's going to be all right, Katie," Mrs. Osborne said. "Don't try to move. The ambulance is coming for you and it's going to be all right."

"Is she dead?" That was Pooch, out of breath, sounding scared. "Is Katie dead?"

"She isn't dead," Mrs. Osborne said. "And she isn't going to die." She sounded sure of that. Katie herself was less certain. She hurt everywhere, especially her leg.

By the time the ambulance arrived, Katie had blacked out again. When she finally opened her eyes, she was in the emergency room of the hospital. Her parents were both there and so were two doctors.

"Your leg is broken," one of the doctors told her, "and you have a dislocated shoulder."

"It's a bad break, Katie-bird," her dad said. "They're going to have to operate on your leg."

He hadn't called her Katie-bird since she was about six years old.

A nurse moved into Katie's line of vision. "This is to make you sleepy," she said, as she gave Katie a shot in the arm.

If she hadn't hurt so much, Katie would have smiled. She'd been unconscious all this time and now that she was finally awake, they were giving her something to make her sleep.

"Just relax," Mrs. Osborne said. "Let yourself go to sleep. When you wake up, the surgery will be over and your leg will be in a cast."

Katie didn't want to go to sleep. She wanted to tell them about the car. She wanted to explain what had happened. But she couldn't. Her tongue felt leaden and her eyes refused to stay open. She heard her mother say something else but the words grew fuzzy and Katie felt herself slipping deep into sleep.

When she awoke, it was dark, except for a dim night-light. The first thing she saw was a bottle, suspended over her shoulder. A tube ran from the bottle to Katie's arm and a clear liquid dripped slowly through the tube.

Katie stared at the bottle a moment, wondering where it came from and what it was doing in her bedroom.

Then she remembered. She wasn't at home, in her own bedroom. She was in the hospital and there was supposed to be a cast on her leg. She started to sit up, to look at her leg, but as soon as she moved, a sharp pain shot through her right shoulder, causing her to gasp.

Immediately, her mother's voice said, "Katie? Are you awake?"

She turned her head toward the voice and saw her mother getting out of a chair beside the bed. She stood beside Katie and put her hand on Katie's forehead.

"How do you feel?" she asked.

"I hurt."

"I'm sure you do. Don't try to move; just lie still."

"Is the cast on my leg?"

"It's there, all right. From your foot, clear up past your knee. Tomorrow I'll buy a box of colored markers so we can all sign it."

Katie didn't answer. A wave of nausea engulfed her and she closed her eyes again while beads of perspiration broke out on her upper lip.

"The nurse will give you something for the pain, whenever you need it," Mrs. Osborne said. There was a small buzzer-type button on Katie's bed, right near her hand, and Mrs. Osborne pressed it. Almost immediately, a nurse came in.

"She's awake," Mrs. Osborne said.

The nurse popped a thermometer in Katie's mouth and took her pulse.

"Does it hurt much?" she asked.

Katie nodded. She didn't want to cry but she couldn't keep the tears from brimming in her eyes. She hurt everywhere, especially her leg.

"I'm going to give you something for the pain," the nurse said. "Any time you need me, just press this call button. It's right beside your hand."

All her life Katie had dreaded getting a shot for anything. This time, she welcomed it—if it would make the pain go away.

She slept then. Later she was vaguely aware of activity from time to time—someone checked the bottle that hung over her, the thermometer was put in her mouth again, another shot. Periodically, she heard the murmur of voices—Mom, a doctor, Dad.

More than once she tried to come up out of her fog but she never quite made it. Each time, the effort to wake up and speak was more than she could manage. Each time, she struggled briefly but lacked the strength.

5

Shannon shivered. It was starting to rain and the drafty old barn offered little protection from the cold, damp air.

Her ankles were raw where the rope had burned them. After the man left on his "business," she tried desperately to get her feet free. If she could just get loose, she could run across the field, even with her hands still tied. If she ran fast enough and far enough, eventually she would find someone to help her.

All she did was ruin her pantyhose and rub the skin off both ankles. She could feel the blood trickle down into her shoes and she was no closer to being free than when she started.

She had to give up. He'd tied her too tightly for her

ever to get away. She wondered where he'd gone. What was so important that he would take a chance of going into town, where he could be recognized. Surely he must realize that by now Katie had given his description to the police. Or maybe he didn't realize it or even think about it.

She still wasn't sure if the man was taking drugs or if he was mentally unbalanced. Maybe it was both. Sometimes he seemed almost normal; other times he seemed completely deranged. Maybe he had a split personality.

The minutes dragged past. Shannon tried to judge the time from the way the shadows moved across the barn floor but the shadows didn't last long. The wind came up and the clouds covered the sun. The bleak grayness of the day matched her mood.

What if he didn't come back? What if he was captured but he wouldn't tell them where she was? What if he couldn't remember? There was no telling what he would say or do. What if he tried to run or pulled his knife on a police officer? He could be shot, killed, and no one would know where Shannon was. She could die here, tied to this post, and her body would never be found.

Stop it, she told herself. There's no point getting all worked up over what might or might not happen. Just stay calm and try to think of something pleasant. Look at the bright side, as her mother was fond of saying. Even her mother, the perpetual optimist, would have a hard time seeing the bright side of this situation.

Shannon wondered what her mother was doing. Was she out looking for Shannon or home, hoping the telephone would ring, waiting for some word from the police. She wouldn't be at work; Shannon was sure of that. She wondered if Dad had gone to work today and if they'd taken Billy to his day care. Probably Dad took time off, to search for her, but there wouldn't be much reason to keep Billy home. A two-year-old would be no help. Billy probably didn't even understand what had happened. He probably didn't know why Shannon wasn't there to read him his bedtime story.

A surge of homesickness brought tears to Shannon's eyes. She might never see her family again. She might never roll out sugar cookie dough with her mother or paddle the canoe up the slough with her dad. She might never again go inside, after playing in the snow on a frosty Sunday afternoon, and be greeted with a steaming mug of hot chocolate.

Her parents weren't perfect and they had a hard time realizing she had a mind of her own but she knew they loved her. They didn't always understand her, but they always loved her.

She loved them, too, and she'd do anything if she

could go home again. Anything! But what could she do?

Shannon looked dejectedly down at the floor. A slight movement caught her attention and she blinked and looked closer. A huge black spider, as big around as a silver dollar, had climbed out from between two loose boards. It had long, fat legs and it was crawling straight toward her.

Shannon hated spiders, even little ones, and this one was bigger than any spider she'd ever seen.

Once, at home, a big spider crawled out of some firewood that Shannon's dad left on the living room floor. When Shannon saw it, she was so horrified, she couldn't even bring herself to step on it. All she could do was scream, throw a magazine on top of it, and run to get her father. He had teased her about it, but for weeks afterward Shannon shuddered whenever she even looked at a piece of firewood.

Now she was looking at an even bigger spider and not only was she unable to squash it, she couldn't run away from it, either.

The spider crawled steadily across the floor; it went up and over a mound of old hay, and headed straight for Shannon's feet. When it came to her foot, it stopped. Shannon stared at it, her eyes wide with apprehension. She began wiggling her shoe, to frighten the spider, but had to stop. Her ankles were already so raw from her earlier struggle that any movement was painful.

The spider crawled slowly up on Shannon's shoe. Her breath came faster. If it comes up my leg, she thought, I will die.

The spider continued across her shoe and then went down to the floor again. Shannon swallowed. She watched as the spider crawled across the floor, up the barn wall, and disappeared into a crack. Only then did her heartbeat return to normal.

It got dark early, because of the rain. Shannon was thirsty again and hungry, and she ached from lying so long on the hard floor of the barn.

She saw the lights of the car before she heard it coming. She strained her ears, hoping to hear more than one engine, hoping to hear the voices of her rescuers.

Instead, she heard one engine stop, one car door slam.

"I brought us a good dinner, Angie," he said. "And a radio. We'll have us some music tonight."

She didn't respond. What could she say? He acted like he was her husband, coming home from work at the end of a perfectly normal day, making chitchat, planning the evening's activities together.

If she told him again that she wasn't Angie, he'd be angry. She decided the best plan was to say as little as possible. At least that way, he wouldn't kick her again.

He pointed his flashlight toward the stack of old

boards. Then he put a portable radio on the floor and turned it on. Country western music filled the barn.

"How do you like that?" he said. "Nice, eh?" He sat down on the boards, tapping his foot to the music.

I should study him, Shannon thought. I should try to remember every detail of what he says and how he acts.

For more than a year now, she had told everyone that she wanted to be a psychiatrist and work with disturbed patients. Most people, especially adults, were impressed when she said that. They expected her to say she wanted to be a teacher or a computer programmer. They never expected her to say she wanted to be a psychiatrist and they treated her with new respect after she said it.

Well, here was her chance to start. Right here in front of her was a living, breathing insane person. She had no doubt about that anymore. Drugs weren't responsible for this man's delusions; his mind simply didn't work right.

She tried to remember the one book she'd read about insanity. It was called *The Psychology of the Insane,* or something like that, and she'd checked it out of the library last summer. She had a hard time getting through all the technical material so she never did read the whole book, but she carried it around with her for six weeks (that was as long as the library would let her keep renewing it) and used it as an excuse to talk about her future career.

One chapter was called "The Irrational Behavior of the Patient." She wished she'd read that one more carefully. It was the easiest part of the book to understand and so she did read it, but she didn't study it or try to memorize any of it. Maybe if she could remember what it said, it would help her now.

She should have practiced those exercises that the Memory Lady recommended. Mr. Gates invited the Memory Lady to give a special presentation to all of his classes one day, on tricks to use to help you remember things. He said if all his students would use the tricks, they'd get better grades in American History.

It was a fun presentation—much better than studying—but Shannon had never seriously tried to use any of the techniques. She did remember some of them, though. One was something the Memory Lady called *visualization*. You were supposed to think back to when you read whatever it was you were trying to remember. She said to picture yourself exactly where you were when you were reading and then imagine yourself reading it again.

"Use details," the Memory Lady said. "Be specific."

Shannon closed her eyes and imagined herself sitting in the brown chair in her living room, with the book in her lap. It was raining outside and she had the table lamp on. The book was large, with a dark blue cover, and she was eating popcorn while she read.

Mentally, she opened the book and turned to the chapter on irrational behavior. Her eyes scanned the page, hoping for something she could understand without needing four years of medical school first.

It clicked in her mind and Shannon opened her eyes, surprised. The memory exercise worked! She could now recall the part of the chapter which had interested her at the time. She didn't remember it word for word but she remembered the important part.

The book said that a patient might think he was someone else—the book used George Washington as an example—and, even when presented with specific, indisputable evidence to the contrary, the patient would continue to believe he was George Washington. No amount of arguing and confronting him with facts would change his mind.

It's true, Shannon realized. I can tell him a thousand times that I'm not Angie. I can show him my cafeteria card with my name on it, to prove I am who I say I am and it isn't going to make any difference. No matter how much proof I have that I am Shannon Lindstrom, he thinks I'm Angie, and nothing is going to change his mind.

Just then, without saying anything, the man came over to her and untied the rope. He didn't say anything about her bleeding ankles; maybe he didn't notice. To her surprise, he also untied her hands. She flexed her arms and legs, feeling the tightness of the cramped muscles.

He'd brought a whole barbecued chicken, the kind you get at the supermarket. When he opened the package, the smell made Shannon's stomach rumble.

Wordlessly, she sat down on the floor next to the stack of boards and broke off a drumstick. It was no longer hot but it tasted wonderful. He sat opposite her and took a piece of chicken, too. She looked in the bag, hoping he'd brought something to drink besides orange soda this time but he hadn't. Once more, she drank only a small amount.

She was gnawing a chicken wing when the music ended.

"In the news tonight," an announcer said, "search parties continue to hunt for Shannon Lindstrom, the twelve-year-old Franklin Middle School student who disappeared yesterday afternoon."

Shannon froze, listening. She looked at the man but he continued to drink his beer, apparently oblivious to what the announcer was saying.

"Shannon's parents, Clyde and Marcia Lindstrom, insist that their daughter would not run away but police have no leads on a possible abductor."

Shannon couldn't believe what she was hearing. What

did they mean, no leads? What about the man who answered the Lindstroms' door yesterday afternoon and made up some story about a piano? Why weren't they broadcasting a description of him?

"Elsewhere in the news," the voice continued, "another twelve-year-old girl was the victim today of a hit-and-run driver. Katie Osborne was struck from behind as she crossed a street near her home. Katie, who was in a pedestrian crosswalk, suffered a compound fracture of her leg, a dislocated shoulder, and possible internal injuries. She is in critical condition tonight at Mountain Community Hospital."

The chicken bone fell from Shannon's fingers. Katie was in the hospital, in critical condition. If she hadn't already given a description of the man to police, she wouldn't be able to do so now. Critical condition meant she was badly hurt, probably unable to talk.

The radio announcer continued, giving other news from around the state, but Shannon no longer listened. Instead, she thought about what she'd just heard. Katie was struck from behind, in a crosswalk, in daylight. It didn't sound very accidental.

A hit-and-run driver. Whoever hit Katie didn't stay to see if she was badly hurt or not. Why not? Maybe the driver hoped she would not be all right. Maybe he thought she was dead. Maybe he wanted her to be dead.

71

The hair on the back of Shannon's neck prickled. Was Katie's accident really an accident—or was it intentional?

The news ended and the music began again. Shannon looked at the man seated across from her, calmly drinking his beer and tapping his foot in time to the music. Why did he leave this afternoon? Where did he go? He kept watching the time, to be sure he left at a certain time. Why?

Could he possibly be the hit-and-run driver? Is that the "business" that took him into town? Did he want to be sure he was driving his car on Katie's street when she walked home from school?

Shannon felt sick. If he *was* the one, it was all her fault. She made such a scene last night. She told him Katie would go to the police, she said Katie would describe him so that they'd be found. How could she have been so stupid? She knew the man was crazy. Why did she say anything about Katie at all?

But she hadn't told him where Katie lived. She couldn't remember the address herself. She hadn't even said Katie's last name.

You're jumping to conclusions, she told herself. It's just a coincidence that Katie was involved in an accident. It has nothing to do with you.

Still, the questions kept flooding Shannon's mind, one after the other. This afternoon was the second time the man had left the barn. He went into town last night, too, while Shannon slept. Did he go to Katie's house then? Had he intended to kill her then and failed?

Shannon wondered if she was getting hysterical. Maybe her imagination was working overtime, thinking that her kidnapper was now trying to kill Katie Osborne. The whole idea was crazy. And yet, Katie was the only person who saw the man at Shannon's house. She was the only one who could identify him as Shannon's kidnapper.

She tried to remember exactly what he'd said while he tied her up. While he was tying her to the post, he explained why he had to go. What did he say?

She might tell. That was it. That's exactly what he said. *She might tell.* Could the "she" be Katie?

Until now, Shannon had pinned her hopes on the certainty that Katie would provide the police with a detailed description of the kidnapper. She was no longer sure that this had happened—or would ever happen.

The idea rekindled Shannon's terror. Who was this man who held her prisoner? What sort of madman was he?

She watched as he nonchalantly lit another cigarette and turned the music louder. If he had tried to kill Katie Osborne this afternoon, he certainly showed no signs of remorse.

She wanted to scream at him, to hit him, to claw him

73

with her fingernails. But she knew violence wouldn't solve her problem. He was far bigger and stronger than she; any physical battle would surely end in catastrophe.

No, her only hope was to outsmart him. He might be stronger than she was but he wasn't any smarter.

The chicken no longer tasted good. Shannon retreated to the far side of the barn and sat down, drawing her knees up under her chin to keep warm. She sat looking at the man, trying to think what to do.

After awhile, he turned off the flashlight and the radio and sat in the doorway, smoking and looking out into the darkness. His cigarette tip glowed in the dark and a pale shaft of moonlight filtered through the window, growing brighter and darker as clouds passed over the moon.

She stared at the cigarette. Maybe he would fall asleep and drop it into the old, dry hay on the barn floor. It happened all the time—a smoker would nod off to sleep while he was smoking in bed and an entire house would burn down.

That would certainly attract some attention, if the old barn should catch fire. The rotting walls were well seasoned; it would catch easily.

A tingle of excitement ran down Shannon's back. Maybe the fire wouldn't have to start accidentally, with a cigarette. Maybe it could be set, on purpose.

She knew he had books of matches; she'd watched him use them. She decided to wait until she was sure he was asleep and then she would set fire to the barn. As soon as it caught, she would run. The bright flames and smoke would probably be seen from miles away. Someone would come.

She lay still, waiting. This time she would not fall asleep first. This time she had to outlast him.

And she did. She saw him put the cigarette out and heard the sounds as he settled himself on the floor, turning and shifting several times to get comfortable.

Shannon waited. His breathing became slower and louder. He wasn't snoring exactly, but she was positive he was asleep. She sat up and began gathering the loose hay into a pile. She needed to be sure she had enough so that the fire would spread quickly.

As she groped in the darkness for more hay, a splinter from the floorboards rammed into her finger, going up under her fingernail. Shannon bit her lip to keep from crying out. She tried to remove the splinter with her other hand but she couldn't see well enough in the dark. She needed a bright light and a pair of tweezers.

She put her finger in her mouth and sucked on it hard, to relieve the pain. She could taste blood and she could also feel the end of the splinter with her tongue. She bit the tip of the splinter, holding hard with her teeth, and jerked it loose.

She felt gingerly for more hay and soon had a pile a foot high and two feet wide. She made it in a corner, where the flames from the hay would leap against two walls. She thought at least one of them would catch.

When she had as much loose hay as she could find, she crept on her hands and knees toward the brown paper bag that the chicken and beer came in. She'd seen him take a book of matches from the bag earlier and she hoped he'd either put it back or that there might be a second book.

One of the old boards creaked as Shannon crawled across it. Quickly she flattened herself and pretended to be asleep. She heard the man stir, and shift position again, but he didn't wake up.

She felt in the darkness for the paper bag, put her hand inside, found a book of matches in the bottom. She removed everything else from the bag, too, and took the bag back to her pile of hay. The paper would make good kindling. She didn't dare crumple it into a ball, as she did with newspapers when she was lighting a fire in the fireplace at home. She was afraid the crumpling of the paper would make too much noise. Instead, she put it on the floor beside the hay pile and pushed some of the dry hay inside the bag.

She knew exactly what she would do. As soon as the fire started to burn, she would tiptoe to the door, step over the sleeping man, and run across the field to freedom. She was counting on his instincts to work in her favor. When he woke up and realized the barn was on fire, she thought his natural tendency would be to try to put the fire out. He might not think about her right away, and she'd get a good head start. Even if he caught up with her, the burning barn would be visible for a long way. Surely someone would come to investigate.

The man's steady breathing continued. Shannon crouched beside the bag of hay, opened the book of matches, and removed one. Her hands were shaking so much that she had a hard time striking it. It took three tries before the match flamed up, brightening her corner of the barn. She glanced at the man. He still slept.

She put the match to the edge of the paper bag and the bag smoked and curled under. She held the match in place, willing the paper to catch. It only smoldered and when the match burned down almost to her fingers, she blew it out.

She struck a second match but this time, instead of holding it to the paper bag, she tossed it directly into the hay inside the bag. It caught immediately and Shannon sprang up, ready to run.

She didn't want to leave too soon. She had to make sure the fire was going to spread and not fizzle out. She leaned over and blew lightly on the flame, encouraging it.

"What the hell are you doing?"

Shannon whirled around. He was behind her, rushing toward her. He caught her by the shoulder and shoved her out of the way. She stumbled, fell, and got back up but before she could reach the door, he had jumped on the fire, crushing it under his boots, putting it out.

Shannon had to make a fast choice. She decided not to run. He would catch her for sure and without the fire to bring help, there was no telling what he would do to her.

She stood there, trembling, as he turned and came back toward her.

"Why did you do that?" he demanded.

She was shaking with fear and disappointment. She said the first thing that popped into her mind. "Because I'm cold."

He reached for her and Shannon cringed but all he did was put his hand on her arm.

"You are, aren't you?" he said and she realized he thought she was shivering from the cold.

The anger faded from his voice. "Poor little Angie," he said. "You should have told me you were cold. You know better than to play with matches. Mother's told you never to play with matches."

"I forgot," Shannon said.

"I'll get the blanket for you," he said. "That'll keep you warm."

He went to the car, brought back the old wool blanket and handed it to her. "Here," he said. "You can wrap up in this."

"Thanks," she said.

"Now don't you be lighting any more fires. It isn't safe. You could have burned this barn down."

How could he change moods so quickly? When he threw her out of his way so he could get to the fire, he was furious. Violent. Now, he was worried about her welfare, making sure she stayed warm.

She carried the blanket back to the far side of the barn, lay down on the floor, and drew the blanket up over her shoulders. Now what?

Setting fire to the barn had been a great idea but it didn't work so she would have to think of something else. She lay still in the darkness and wondered what to try next.

6

The bottle was gone.

Until now, that was the first thing Katie saw, each time she opened her eyes: the bottle of liquid suspended in the air above her, with its long, slender tube attached to her arm.

Katie blinked and looked around the stark, white room. For the first time, she saw it clearly, rather than through a haze of pain.

It was morning. Sunshine streamed through the window, spotlighting the small bedside table with its blue plastic water bottle, a small box of tissues, and a white wicker basket containing an African violet. The violet was covered with lavender blossoms, Katie's favorite color. A gift card was wedged between two of the leaves.

Curious, she reached for the card and read it. "Mend fast," it said. "Love, Linda, Mark, and Sammy."

She didn't remember receiving a plant. Dimly she remembered waking several times, trying to move, crying out from the pain, getting another shot, going back to sleep.

Her leg still hurt but now it was a hurt she could live with. It was an aspirin kind of hurt, not a please-give-me-another-shot-because-I-can't-stand-the-pain kind of hurt.

She cautiously raised herself up on one elbow, lifted the blanket and sheet, and looked at her leg. The cast was white as a refrigerator and heavy looking. She would not be participating in P.E. at Franklin for awhile, that's for sure.

Shannon! Thinking about school, made her remember Shannon. She wondered what had happened, if Shannon was back home yet.

Her thoughts were interrupted by a nurse, who bustled into the room and said cheerfully, "Well! I see we're awake. Would we like some breakfast this morning?"

"Yes, I would," Katie said. A Pekinese, she thought. The nurse looked like a Pekinese, with her round face, stubby nose and short, fat legs. Katie liked Pekinese. They had good dispositions and she thought the way their chubby rear ends waddled when they walked was funny.

81

The nurse left the room and Katie watched her leave, trying not to laugh. Yes, she thought. This one's definitely a Pekinese.

She'd just finished eating a dish of oatmeal when her mother arrived, bringing a bouquet of lavender helium balloons, which she tied to the end of Katie's bed.

"Your leg is going to heal nicely," Mrs. Osborne said, "and so is your shoulder, but you gave us quite a scare. It's a compound fracture so it'll be awhile before you get the cast off but compared to what might have happened, I guess you're lucky."

Katie nodded. She didn't feel terribly lucky at the moment, but she knew what her mother meant. At least she was here; she was alive.

"How did it happen?" Mrs. Osborne said. "It isn't like you to walk out in front of a car without looking."

"I—I'm not sure," Katie said. "I didn't see any car coming. I didn't hear it, either, until it was right on top of me."

"It was a hit-and-run," Mrs. Osborne said. "Did you know that? The driver never stopped. He—or she— left you lying there in the street."

There was a cold, steely sound to her mother's voice, a tone that Katie had never heard before. She's furious, Katie realized. She's plain furious at that driver for going off and leaving me there.

"The police want to question you, as soon as you feel

up to it," Mrs. Osborne continued. "They hope you might remember something about the car. So far, they have no idea who the driver was."

"I don't remember much," Katie said.

"I'm not surprised, after what you've been through."

"Have they found Shannon Lindstrom yet?" Katie asked.

"Who? Oh, the girl who's missing. Do you know her?"

"She's in one of my classes and I sat with her at lunch on Tuesday. I was wondering if she's been found yet."

"No. There was a picture of her in last night's paper and there are Search and Rescue teams looking for her, but I don't think they've found anything yet."

A doctor arrived to check Katie and he said she should try getting up for awhile. She had to learn to use crutches before she could go home.

The first time she put her legs over the side of the bed and sat up, she nearly fainted. Until then, the injured leg had been propped up on pillows. When she put her foot down, all the blood rushed to her leg, causing it to throb painfully.

With the Pekinese nurse on one side and her mother on the other side, she managed to stand up, using a crutch under each arm.

"Don't try to walk this first time," the nurse said. "We'll just have you stand for a few moments. You can try walking later this afternoon."

That was fine with Katie. She didn't think she could walk if the room was on fire.

"I feel so weak," she said. "And kind of dizzy."

"Your body's been through a terrible trauma," Mrs. Osborne said. "It will take awhile to recover."

Lieutenant Collins from the Franklin Police Department stopped to see Katie that afternoon. He introduced himself and then asked her to tell him everything she could remember about the accident. "Take your time," he said. "Think about exactly how you were walking and where you were going. Tell me everything you remember, even little details that you don't think are important."

"I was going home from school," Katie said, "and I came to the corner where my friend Shannon turned off the day before. I was thinking about her—about her being missing—and feeling sad and hoping she'd be found and that she was OK."

Lieutenant Collins wrote something in the small notebook he held but he didn't say anything. He just smiled at Katie and nodded.

"I went on past her corner," Katie continued, "and started to go across the street. I didn't see the car coming. I didn't hear it, either, until the last second and then it seemed loud, like it was going fast, and it was right behind me. I tried to jump out of the way and at the same time, I turned to look."

She hesitated, frowning. She did see the car at the last moment, a blur of green coming at her, and she jumped forward, trying to get out of the way. It had all happened so fast that she couldn't be positive but, as she recreated the scene in her memory, Katie felt the car had swerved toward her. Instead of slamming on the brakes and pulling the car away from her, it seemed the driver had stepped on the gas and aimed straight for Katie's back.

She wasn't certain that's what happened. It was over before she had much chance to react and yet, instinctively, she knew that the driver had not tried to avoid hitting her. If anything, he'd done just the opposite. Should she tell the officer that? She didn't want to sound like a hysterical person or have him think she was trying to make more out of the accident than she should, as a way to get attention.

"Go on, Katie," Lieutenant Collins said. "You were saying you tried to jump out of the way and you turned to look at the car. What did you see?"

"I think it was green," Katie said.

"What else? Don't be afraid to tell me, even if you aren't sure of what you remember."

"Well," Katie said, "I have the feeling the car could have turned away from me but instead it came right at me. It's almost like—like the driver *wanted* to hit me. I know that sounds stupid but that's how it seems."

"It doesn't sound stupid," Lieutenant Collins said. "That might be exactly what happened."

"But why would someone want to hit me? Nobody would try to hit a person."

"Most hit-and-runs are caused by people on alcohol or drugs. Their judgment is so severely impaired that often they don't realize they've hit someone. That's why they don't stop. Can you remember anything else about the car? Anything at all?"

Katie shook her head. "After it hit me, I didn't see anything else."

"Too bad there wasn't someone else in the area," Lieutenant Collins said. "One witness is all we need; one person who could describe the car and, possibly, the driver. But it seems you were the only one on the street just then."

"Who found me?" Katie asked. She hadn't thought of that before. She wondered how long she'd lain in the street before someone came along.

"Two boys on bicycles. They ran to the closest house and got help."

"It all seems like a bad dream," Katie said.

"You're lucky to be alive," Lieutenant Collins said. "If we find the driver, we'll throw the book at him. Knowing the car was green is a big help to us. We've already alerted all the auto repair shops in the area to be watching for a car with damage to the front end, especially if there's any sign of blood or fragments of clothing."

Katie was glad she could remember something useful. Even though the car had been a blur, she was certain of the color. She was sure it was green.

"Were you and Shannon Lindstrom close friends?" Lieutenant Collins asked.

"I only met her Tuesday. That was my first day at the Franklin school and Shannon and I walked partway home together."

"Was that immediately after school?"

Katie nodded. "She asked me to go shopping with her but I couldn't go because I had to take care of my brother and when I went to her house to tell her I couldn't go, she wasn't home."

"What time was that?"

"About four o'clock."

"What did you do then?"

"I went back home."

"Did you talk to Shannon after that?"

"No. I was going to call her but we had company."

"When did you learn that she was missing?"

"The next morning, at school. Mr. Gates announced it to our class and said if anyone knew where Shannon was, they should tell."

"As you walked home together, did anyone approach you? Did either of you talk to anyone?"

"No," Katie said. Did he think she was a baby with no sense? Indignantly she added, "I know not to talk to strangers and I'm sure Shannon does, too."

Lieutenant Collins stood up and put his notebook in his pocket. "Thanks for your help, Katie," he said. "You'll hear from me if we find the driver of the car that hit you."

"I hope you find Shannon, too," Katie said.

"We're doing our best."

I wish I could help, Katie thought, after Lieutenant Collins left. If she could walk, she'd volunteer to be on one of the search teams.

If there was something she could do that would help find her new friend, she'd gladly do it. Anything! But she had no idea what she could do. Especially when she was stuck in the hospital with a broken leg.

7

It was time to begin.

Shannon didn't know if her plan would work or not, but she had to try something. She couldn't just sit there in the barn forever, waiting for someone to find them. It was time to put Part One of her plan into action.

She'd fashioned a makeshift broom out of some long weeds and she was energetically sweeping the spot where they always sat when they ate. She didn't hope to actually get it clean but she needed something to do with her hands and she was trying to create a homey feeling, to get the man to relax and talk to her.

He sat in the doorway of the barn, where he always sat, leaning back against the rotting wooden doorframe, watching her.

She winced as she accidentally brushed her foot with the broom. Her ankles were still sore from when she'd rubbed them raw trying to get loose, two days ago, while the man was in town.

Since then, the minutes had crawled by. Shannon spent all day Thursday listening in vain for the sound of a car approaching or a helicopter overhead—*any* indication that she was going to be found. The man, meanwhile, gave no hint of his plans. He seemed content just to sit there, looking out the door, doing nothing.

Until now, Shannon had tried to be patient. She didn't want to provoke him again and she kept hoping they'd be found. But now, she couldn't stand it any longer. She had to do something.

"My mind's just a blank this morning," she said, trying to sound casual, as she whisked the broom back and forth. "Ever since I woke up, I've been trying to think what it was I used to call you. You know, the name I always used when we were together. Seems to me there was a special nickname but I just can't remember."

"I don't remember any nickname," he said.

"You don't? I wonder what I'm thinking of then. What did I always call you, when we were together?"

Shannon held her breath, though she continued sweeping. She didn't dare to look at him. Would he realize what she was doing?

"You always called me David, as far as I can recollect."

She let out her breath. So far, so good. She knew his first name now and that was a start. David.

He scowled at her. "Seems odd that you can't remember your own brother's name."

"Don't be silly," Shannon said. "Of course, I know your name. I just thought I used to call you by a nickname sometimes, when I was little."

Your own brother. So that was it. He thought she was his sister, Angie. She wondered what Angie looked like. The man had reddish hair, much like Shannon's. She supposed it was possible that she did resemble his sister.

She tried to remember what he'd said that first night, about wanting to find her and being sure she'd wait for him at home. None of it had made any sense to her at the time. Now she decided to try to piece together the puzzle.

"How did you know where to find me?" she asked.

He looked surprised. "I just figured you'd be home, like always."

"But it's been a long time since you saw me. Can you even remember the address?"

"Thirteen forty-two Elmhurst Drive," he said. "How could I forget that?"

Shannon blinked at him and stopped sweeping. He

said the address without hesitation, as if he really did live there himself. But that was crazy! The Lindstroms bought the house three years ago, when Shannon's mother was expecting Billy and they needed more space. And the people they bought the house from were elderly, a retired couple with no children. She couldn't remember how long they said they'd lived there but she thought it was a long time.

"I can't remember moving into that house," Shannon said. That wasn't true, of course. She remembered it perfectly but she had to keep David talking if she was ever going to learn anything.

"Of course, you don't," he said. "You were only a year old. I was just three myself." He smiled at her. It was the first time she'd seen him smile. Maybe her plan was going to work. "I love our house," he said. "Especially my room. I like the way the ceiling slopes and the window seat that looks down into the weeping willow."

Shannon nodded, feeling numb. He was describing her bedroom.

"How did you get in?" she asked. "The other day, I mean, when you were waiting for me to get home. The doors were locked. How did you get the door open?"

"I didn't use the door. I used the bathroom window. Remember how it never quite closed all the way? Whenever we'd forget to take a key and we'd be locked out, I always climbed in that way." He shrugged. "I just did it again."

It was true. The window in the downstairs bathroom didn't close properly. Shannon's dad had mentioned it once. He meant to fix it but somehow it didn't get done.

Shannon smiled cheerfully at him. I should win an Oscar for this performance, she thought. She tried to think what else he'd said, that first night. Something about an accident.

"What do you remember about the accident?" she asked.

He was quiet for so long, she thought he hadn't heard her. "I don't remember the accident myself," she said, trying to prod him. "What happened?"

He jumped to his feet and started toward her. Shannon dropped the broom in alarm and stepped away from him. His eyes were wild again, darting back and forth. Abruptly, he turned away from her and went the other way. He was pacing again, back and forth, back and forth.

"We were going home," he said, his voice so low she had to strain to hear it. "You and Mother and me. We were playing a game in the car, the alphabet game, and you kept asking if we could stop for ice cream. And then the other car crossed over the line and came right at us. Mother screamed and I looked up just as the car crashed into us. I hit my head on the dashboard."

His hand went up to touch the scar. Shannon didn't move.

"I heard you crying and crying and I told Mother you were hurt but she didn't answer me. I put my hand on her hand, to get her attention, and I looked at her face and I knew she was dead." His voice broke. "Mother was dead."

Shannon didn't speak. She stood quietly, watching him pace, afraid to say anything.

"Some people came to help us but by then you'd stopped crying. They took me to a hospital and later Aunt Betty came and took me to her house. She told me Mother went to heaven and took you with her but I knew she was lying. You didn't die in the accident. I heard you crying."

He stopped pacing and stood facing her with tears in his eyes, his hands hanging helplessly.

"How old were you?" Shannon whispered.

"Fourteen."

She did some quick arithmatic. If Angie was one when David was three, then Angie would have been twelve when David was fourteen. Just the age Shannon was now.

David began pacing again. "I kept trying to go back home, to get you, and they kept going after me. And then one day Aunt Betty told me I was going to live somewhere else. She said the people there would try to help me get well. I didn't know what she was talking about. I wasn't sick. But she said I had to go anyway. She drove me there and took me inside, and then she left and the doors were locked. I tried to run after her and I couldn't because the doors were locked." His voice was getting louder; he was nearly shouting at her. "I was locked in and I couldn't get out! I couldn't get home to find you."

He reached down, picked up an empty beer can, and hurled it at the wall. It struck with such force that it bounced back again, halfway across the barn. David ran to it and kicked it, viciously, again and again. He followed it back and forth across the barn, each time kicking it as hard as he could.

Shannon didn't know what to do. She cowered against the wall, hoping he wouldn't notice her. She hadn't meant to trigger an outbreak like this. She knew for sure now that his bizarre behavior was not caused by drugs. He was crazy, completely out of his mind. Maybe his brain was injured when he hit his head on the dashboard. Or maybe he just went nuts from losing his mother and his sister at the same time. It must have been horrible for him.

Clearly, he'd been a mental patient for a long time. She wondered how old he was. Twenty-two? Twenty-three, maybe? If he was fourteen when the accident happened, that meant he'd been in a mental institution for at least eight years. Had it helped him at all? She wondered if he had been released or if he'd escaped.

How could he think Angie would still be twelve years old, after all this time? Did he still think he was fourteen?

Slowly, she inched away from him until her back hit the side of the barn. She sat down and said nothing. He was crying now, sobbing uncontrollably as he continued to kick the beer can back and forth.

I want to go home, Shannon thought. I don't want to be here with him one more minute.

She thought about how her mother used to tuck her into bed when she was sick and bring her glasses of juice and ask her if she needed anything else. That's what she wanted right now—to be home, in her own bed, and have her mom there to give her a glass of juice.

She remembered once when her mom brought her apple juice and she whined because she wanted root beer instead. Right now, she'd give most anything for a big glass of apple juice. It wouldn't even have to be cold. Except for the chicken, she'd had nothing but junk food for three days, with orange soda to drink. A fresh apple or a big green salad sounded like heaven.

Shannon put her head down on her knees. She wondered if she would ever have a decent meal again.

After awhile, his sobs subsided and he quit kicking the beer can around. Shannon lifted her head and watched him. He returned to the barn door, sat down in his usual place, and lit a cigarette. He sat for hours, just smoking and looking at the sky. The time dragged so that Shannon thought she'd go crazy, too. But she was afraid to move, afraid to say anything, for fear of triggering another outburst.

Finally, for no apparent reason, he stood up, picked up a box of cookies, and passed them to her. Shannon took one. "Thanks," she said.

"It's nice and peaceful here, isn't it?" he said.

"It sure is."

He sounded calm again, the way he'd been this morning before she started questioning him.

"This is the kind of place I want us to get," he said. "Away from people, where it's quiet. In the evenings, you can play the piano for me, like you used to. And we'll get us a cat."

"A little farm," Shannon said. "For just the two of us."

He closed his eyes, a faint smile on his face.

Now, Shannon thought. Now, while he looks so calm. If the second part of the plan is going to work, this is the time to try it.

She took a deep breath, walked over to the doorway, and sat down beside him. Not too close, but near enough so she could plainly see his face. She wanted to be sure how he reacted before she pushed it. After what happened this morning, she didn't want to press her luck.

"You know what I need, David?" she said. "I need to take a shower."

He opened his eyes and nodded at her, as if he understood, but he said nothing.

"I was thinking," she continued, "that we could drive to the state park. I went camping there a few times with the Girl Scouts and there are hot showers for 25¢. We could stop somewhere first and buy some soap."

He watched her silently. She decided to try a different approach.

"Doesn't your hair feel greasy?" she said. "Mine does. And my head itches. Wouldn't it feel good to shampoo your hair and have a shower and get all clean?"

He put one hand up and ran it through his hair.

"I don't know how far we are from the state park," Shannon said, "but it can't be too far. I bet we could find it."

"I don't have a towel," he said.

"We can use the blanket. It's not as good as a towel but it would work. We could take turns."

"Turns?"

"Yes. You can go first. Take the blanket with you into the men's shower room and then when you've dried yourself with it and are dressed again, you can give the blanket to me and I'll go in the women's shower room."

It wouldn't happen like that, of course. If he agreed to this plan and went into the men's shower, she would not be there waiting for him when he came out. Not on your life. She'd be long gone to the ranger's station or to the first group of campers she could find, to tell them who she was and to telephone the police.

"Well . . ."

Her heart began to race. He was considering it. He was actually thinking of taking her to the state park.

"Let's do it, David," she said. "And then after we get clean we can come back here and decide what we're going to do next, where we're going to live. We can't stay here all winter. It's too cold. Maybe we can look around, find a little farm like you talked about."

His eyes narrowed and he cocked his head to one side, examining her. Had she gone too far? She should have quit with the shower. That's all she wanted, anyway. If she could talk him into doing that, she didn't have to worry about what would happen next. She would be able to escape at the state park; she was sure of it.

"All right," he said. "A shower would feel good."

Shannon tried not to show her excitement as she gathered up the blanket and stepped outside to shake it. It was dirty and pieces of old hay stuck to it, no matter how hard she shook. Hardly what she'd choose to dry herself with after a shower. She folded it into a square and tucked it under her arm.

"Ready?" she said and, to her relief, David stood up and started toward the car.

Shannon hadn't been near the car since they first arrived at the barn. Both times when David went to town and returned, he parked a hundred feet or so away from the barn door, behind one of the trees. As they headed in that direction now, Shannon decided she would memorize David's license number. That way, if she was able to escape, she could give it to the police.

HES-211. She knew she'd have a better chance of remembering it if she made up something for the letters and numbers to stand for. That was another of the Memory Lady's tricks, to make up a slogan for letters and a date for numbers. HES-211. The 211 was easy. Billy was born on February 11; all she had to do was remember Billy's birthday. And the H-E-S could stand for Hogs Eat Slop. Hogs Eat Slop and Billy's birthday. She could remember both of those.

As Shannon crossed in front of the car, she noticed that one of the front headlights was broken. She looked closer and saw that there was something caught in the fragmented glass. It looked like a piece of cloth.

She started to pick it off and then drew her hand back. Maybe the cloth was torn from Katie's clothing.

She shuddered. The car seemed so big and there were so many hard pieces of metal. How would it feel to get knocked over by something so hard? She left the piece of cloth untouched. If David was the hit-and-run driver, any evidence should be left right where it was. If her plan worked, the police would see it soon.

He started the engine and pulled the car forward through the long weeds, onto what once might have been a road. The weeds were bent down now, where the car had previously gone in and out. David followed his own tracks.

The radio came on when he turned on the engine and Shannon was glad when he didn't turn it off. She hadn't heard a news broadcast since the day before yesterday because David had decided he liked it better in the barn when it was quiet. She wondered if her disappearance was still newsworthy enough to be mentioned or if she'd been replaced by other, more current happenings.

It didn't matter. If she could get David to leave her alone while he went to take a shower, she'd be free anyway. *That* would make the news, if she escaped from him in the state park and ran for help.

They left the bumpy, weed-covered field and turned onto a narrow two-lane road. She didn't recognize anything. She still had no idea where they were. Scrubby trees grew alongside the road, some of them so close that their branches brushed against the car window. Clearly, the road was seldom used.

In a few miles, they turned again, onto a wider road. She saw a grove of trees ahead, with a long lane running beside them. There was a mailbox at the end of the lane so she knew there must be a farmhouse somewhere back in the trees, at the end of the lane. She felt better, knowing there were other people nearby.

Soon they passed an old school, its windows boarded up and its playground equipment rusty and falling apart. She remembered passing it before, long ago, with her parents. She thought the road they were on now would lead into Franklin.

He drove erratically, speeding for awhile and then going so slowly that once a man on a bicycle actually passed them, on the right. Shannon hoped the cyclist would turn and look in the car. She pressed her forehead against the window, wanting him to see her entire face and not just her profile. If he looked at her, she would mouth the word, "Help." Maybe he'd even recognize her as the girl who was missing. But the cyclist put his head down, leaned forward over the handlebars, and passed them without a glance.

A short time later, David accelerated again, passed the bicycle, and left it far behind.

She began to see signs advertising various businesses in Franklin and she knew they were approaching the town. Two cars passed them, going the opposite direction. Her mouth felt dry and she chewed nervously on one lip.

"There it is!" she cried, pointing toward the green highway sign. "Clover State Park, 1 mile." An arrow pointed to the right and David turned at the intersection.

It all looked familiar now. Shannon remembered the road through the trees and the bridge over the stream. The ranger's house should be just ahead on the left and not far past that was the big sign that explained the rules and fees for overnight camping.

She saw smoke from a campfire and heard a dog barking, so she knew there were people camping in the park. She should have no trouble finding someone to help her.

They had just passed the ranger's house when the music on the radio ended and a news broadcast began. The announcer gave some headlines from around the world but Shannon didn't pay much attention. She was looking ahead, watching for the concrete building which housed the rest rooms and showers.

"In local news," the announcer said, "Katie Osborne, the twelve-year-old hit-and-run victim, has been discharged from Mountain Community Hospital. Police are still searching for the driver who struck Katie as she crossed the street near her home."

David's foot hit the brake. The tires screeched and Shannon's head jerked forward with a snap. He reached in his pants' pocket, took out a crumpled slip of paper, and looked at it.

It was a scrap of notebook paper, with some penciled writing. Shannon leaned toward him until she could read what it said.

Katie Osborne   328-0677
235 Chestnut St.

David stuffed the paper back into his pocket and made a U-turn.

"Where are you going?" Shannon said. "The showers are just ahead, David. Don't you want your nice, hot shower?"

"Shut up!" he said. His voice was completely different from what it was when he agreed to drive to the state park. He sounded now the way he sounded when he first kidnapped her and held the knife over her and kicked her. Harsh. Mean. Determined.

He wasn't going to go into the men's shower room and leave her outside, to escape. It wasn't going to happen. She'd planned it so carefully, pretending to be Angie so she would gain his confidence, and now her plan had failed. All because of the stupid news broadcast on the radio. If he hadn't heard the news just then, he would have stopped at the showers. Now, instead of stopping in the park, he was going to go after Katie again. She was almost sure of it. But what about her? What did he plan to do with her?

He turned left out of the state park road, headed away from town, back the way they'd come. Shannon felt sick with disappointment. He was taking her back to the barn. She didn't think she could stand it if he tied her up again and left her there to wait for him. How long could this go on?

She had to get away. She had to get help, had to warn someone that he was trying to kill Katie. She didn't know what had happened that first night when David went into town but on his second time to go after Katie, he had nearly succeeded. He could not be given another chance.

Her mind raced, trying to think what to do, how to stop him.

Maybe she could get him talking again, get him thinking about something else. He might forget about Katie if she could get his thoughts on something completely different. She didn't know if it would work or not. He was so unstable, there was no way to guess his reaction to anything but she had to try something. She couldn't just ride meekly back to the barn and get out and let him tie her up again.

She decided to stop pretending she was Angie. Maybe that would shake him up, take his mind off Katie. She would try a whole new approach.

"What's the best thing that ever happened to you?" Shannon asked. She tried to smile, tried to look casual, as if this was an ordinary conversation between friends.

He looked sideways at her, said nothing, and continued to drive too fast, swerving frequently across the center line and back. She wondered how he ever got his driver's license, the way he drove, and then realized he probably didn't have one. The car might be stolen, for all she knew. She hoped it was. The police would be looking for it, if it was reported as stolen.

"I think the best thing that ever happened to me," she continued, "was when I won $25 for writing an essay on 'I Believe in Freedom.' I got a certificate, too, and got my name in the paper. It was pretty exciting. Did you ever win anything?"

"No."

"Something good must have happened to you."

"No good things, only bad. And the worst was getting locked up." He spoke too loudly, as if he were announcing it to the world rather than just telling her. A nerve throbbed in his neck and his knuckles whitened as he clenched the steering wheel.

She shouldn't have talked to him. She shouldn't have said anything at all. She'd meant to calm him down and make him forget about Katie. Instead, she'd made him more tense than ever.

106

"I'm never going back!" he cried. "I won't let her tell them where we are!"

The wild, animal-like expression was in his eyes again. If he weren't seated in the car, she knew he'd be pacing. She'd never seen anyone so changeable. In his present state of mind, she knew he was perfectly capable of killing Katie. Shannon had no doubt at all now that David had driven into town, found Katie's house, waited for Katie to come home from school, and then intentionally run her down. And left her for dead.

Yet, she'd glimpsed a tenderness in him, too, when he was remembering his childhood. And he was capable of deep love and loyalty, where Angie was concerned. She was quite sure he would risk his own life for Angie.

Shannon leaned her head against the back of the seat and closed her eyes, trying not to cry. She was exhausted. For three days, she hadn't eaten properly, hadn't slept well, had spent her time trying to outguess a maniac and now she was no closer to escape than she'd been at the start.

Maybe she should just go along with him. Do whatever he said. He couldn't keep her there in the barn forever. If nothing else, he was bound to run out of money sooner or later and then he'd be forced to do something different in order to have food and gasoline. But how long would that take? She had no idea how much money he had. For all she knew, they could subsist on orange soda and potato chips for weeks. Months.

And what about Katie? No matter how tired she was, Shannon knew she couldn't allow herself to be tied in the barn, knowing that David was going into town to kill Katie.

She couldn't give up. She couldn't! She had to do something.

She opened her eyes and looked out the window. She saw the old school and realized they were nearing the corner where David would turn off this road, onto the narrow, little-used two-lane road that led toward the abandoned barn. If she was going to make a move, she had to do it soon.

He was driving slowly again, and he kept going first onto the shoulder of the road and then back across the center line. Shannon looked at the speedometer. He was doing only twenty miles an hour. She didn't think she could kill herself if she jumped out when they were only going twenty miles an hour.

The grove of trees and the lane with the mailbox were just ahead. If she was lucky, she wouldn't break any bones. She could run to the farmhouse before David caught her. She'd have a head start because he'd have to turn the car around before he could chase her.

But what if there was no one home at the farm-house? What if she couldn't get in and David caught her?

There was no time to think of an alternate plan. As the mailbox came into view, Shannon put her hand on the door handle. When the car was almost even with the grove of trees, she jerked the handle back and jumped.

8

It was hard not to feel sorry for herself. Katie looked out the hospital window at the gray mist and wished she were back in Mill Valley. The sun was probably shining in Mill Valley.

She turned her head on the pillow and looked around the room. The balloons were still tied to the end of her bed but the strings looped limply toward the floor and the balloons looked like they were fast losing their ability to stay aloft. The basket of African violets still bloomed on the bedside table but they didn't lift her spirits. They were from her family. It was expected that her own family would send her something.

What Katie longed for was some attention from her friends. When Bitsy had her appendix out last year, all of the kids visited her in the hospital and the window ledge was lined with get-well cards and she got so many boxes of candy that she even passed it around to the nurses. If Katie were hospitalized in Mill Valley, she wouldn't be lying here all alone, bored half to death, with no one to talk to.

Ever since the move, nothing had gone right. Katie knew this wasn't true but that's how she felt. Her leg still ached and so did her shoulder and when she looked in the mirror this morning for the first time since the accident, she saw the huge red mark on her face, where her cheek slid across the concrete.

The doctor said the skin would grow back and she wouldn't have a scar but Katie wasn't sure if he was telling the truth. She looked like she'd be disfigured for life. Ugly. That's how she looked. Ugly, like a pit bull. Maybe it's a good thing she didn't have any company. She didn't particularly want anyone to see her like this.

She'd had visitors last night, of course. Mark offered to watch both Sammy and Pooch so that Linda could come with her parents to the hospital. Pooch was outraged because visitors under ten years of age were not allowed.

As it turned out, the visit would have been more fun if Linda had stayed home. They'd been there only a short time and Mr. Osborne was trying to make Katie laugh by telling some silly joke he'd heard at work that day, when Linda complained of stomach cramps. Immediately, Mr. and Mrs. Osborne shifted their concern from Katie to Linda and they left way before visiting hours were over because they agreed that Linda needed to go home and lie down.

Katie knew it wasn't Linda's fault that she kept getting sick but still, she would be glad when her sister's baby was finally born and things could get back to normal. Ever since they moved and Linda and Mrs. Osborne could talk daily on the telephone, it seemed to Katie that the whole household revolved around Linda's pregnancy. It was Linda this and the doctor said that, blah, blah, blah. Katie was sick and tired of the whole business.

Mrs. Osborne had said she'd be back to visit Katie this afternoon. Linda wouldn't be coming again but Katie didn't mind. It wasn't Linda she wanted to see, anyway. She wanted her friends. She wanted to talk about school and basketball games and the latest movies.

She sighed. She wondered how many years it would take before she had any friends in Franklin.

The Pekinese nurse bustled into the room. "Are we ready to try using our crutches again?" she said.

"I guess so," Katie said. She'd done quite well with the crutches last night, despite the pain in her shoulder.

"Doctor said if we can walk with no problems again

112

this morning, we might be able to go home today."

"We might?" Katie said. "I mean, *I* might?" She brightened. She had thought she'd have to stay at least another day.

Pekinese lowered her voice, as if to tell Katie a great secret. "Most broken legs stay longer," she said, "but since our mother's a nurse Doctor says we'll get good care at home." Her voice dropped even lower. "Besides, the hospital's overcrowded."

That was certainly good news. Katie was lonely here and she much preferred her mother's cooking to the hospital food. Maybe Mom would fix spaghetti and French bread, Katie's favorite dinner. And chocolate pudding with real whipped cream on it.

And if she didn't get any people visitors, at least she'd have Fred to keep her company. Usually, Fred slept in his dog basket but when she was sick, he was allowed to get up on her bed. Fred loved it when she was sick enough to stay in bed all day. He always snuggled up as close as he could get and spent the day in bed, too.

Pekinese stayed beside Katie, ready to catch her if she needed help, but Katie managed alone. Her shoulder didn't hurt as much this time and she was able to go almost to the end of the hall and back.

The crutches still seemed awkward and she couldn't move very fast but Pekinese assured her it would get easier with practice.

The last few feet back toward the bed were a real

effort. "Whew," Katie said, as she sank back against the pillow. "I feel like I just ran the Boston Marathon."

"We always feel weak, after surgery," Pekinese said.

When the doctor came, he checked Katie and read her chart. "I think we'll send you home today," he said. "You can call your mother and tell her you can leave any time after two."

"I'll tell her 2:01," Katie said.

Mrs. Osborne arrived promptly at two.

"The mail truck came just as I was leaving," she said and she handed Katie an envelope.

While her mother went to the business office to sign Katie out, Katie eagerly opened the long-awaited letter from Bitsy.

Dear Katie, the letter began. *You won't believe what has happened. It's so fantastic I can't believe it myself. Gordon McDowell stopped me after Spanish and asked me to go to a movie with him Friday night. He was wearing . . .*

Katie skimmed quickly down the page. She didn't care what clothes Gordon the Greyhound wore. She wanted to know what was happening at Mill Valley School. How was the basketball team doing? Did Mary Louise get any of her poems published in the school paper yet? Was Miss Sanderson still as grumpy as ever?

But the whole letter was about Gordon McDowell. What he said, what Bitsy said, how he looked at her. It was disgusting.

At the very end there was a P.S.: *There's a new girl in our grade. Her name is Suzanne and she plays violin in the orchestra. I'm spending the night at her house on Saturday.*

Lucky Suzanne, Katie thought, as she stuffed the letter back in the envelope. She'll get to hear every detail of the big Friday night date.

Katie knew she shouldn't be angry at Bitsy but she couldn't help it. She'd looked forward to getting mail and now she felt more alone than she did before she read the letter. Bitsy not only had the boyfriend she wanted, it appeared she also had a new girlfriend, to take Katie's place. Life in Mill Valley was moving along just fine without Katie. Nobody even missed her.

She sighed. She had no choice but to make a new life for herself here in Franklin. But it sure wasn't going to be easy.

Katie left her hospital room in a wheelchair, feeling self-conscious. She held the African violet in her lap while she was pushed grandly down the hall, into the elevator, across the lobby and out to the curb, where her mother's car was parked.

Getting transferred from the wheelchair to the car was no simple task but she finally made it after bumping her cast once on the car door and wincing from the pain. She didn't say anything, though. She didn't want to risk having them change their minds about releasing her.

She felt strange all the way home, as if she were returning from a long journey. The accident had happened on Wednesday and this was only Friday. Just forty-eight hours, but if felt more like forty-eight days.

Fred went crazy when she came in. He yipped high, excited little yips and ran around in circles. Mrs. Osborne had to put him out; she was afraid Katie would trip on him.

"He can come back in after you're safely in bed," she said.

Her own bed felt wonderful and Katie was only too happy to get in it. She didn't see how she could lose much energy in only two days but the effort of getting in and out of the car and the ride home had left her completely worn out.

She was glad she'd let her mother convince her to leave her pajamas on under her coat, rather than getting dressed to come home. All she had to do when she got there was remove one shoe and sock and slip between the sheets. Gratefully, she put her head back and closed her eyes.

"Are you awake?" Pooch said from the bedroom doorway.

Katie tried to clear the fog out of her brain and open her eyes.

"Are you awake?" he said again, louder this time.

Groggily, Katie opened her eyes and blinked at him. He was standing in the doorway of her room with Fred, watching her sleep.

"SHE'S AWAKE, MOM," Pooch yelled and then he and Fred both dashed toward her.

Fred jumped on the bed, licked Katie enthusiastically on the arm, and flopped down beside her. She could tell he liked this arrangement already.

"Did your leg hurt a lot when it broke?" Pooch asked, "Did the bones stick out through your skin? Did you have to use a bedpan?"

"Don't pester Katie with a lot of questions, Pooch," Mrs. Osborne said as she joined them. "She may not feel like talking."

"That's OK," Katie said. "I feel better now that I've slept a little."

"You slept *a lot*," Pooch declared. "I've been waiting for you to wake up for hours and hours."

"You have?" Katie said. "What time is it?"

"It's 3:45," Mrs. Osborne said. "Pooch got home from school about ten minutes ago."

"Mom said you got fed through your veins the first day, instead of in your mouth," Pooch said. "Is that true?"

"That's right," Katie said.

"Where did they do it?" he asked.

"In my left arm." She pushed up the sleeve of her

pajama and showed him the black-and-blue mark on the inside of her elbow, where the intravenous needle had been inserted.

Pooch stared at the mark for a long moment. Then he said, "I see the place but I still don't see how they got the spoon in."

Mrs. Osborne explained how the liquid nourishment drips from a bottle suspended over the patient's bed, down a tube, and through a needle which has been inserted in the vein.

"You mean they gave you a shot and left the needle *in* you?" Pooch cried.

"Taped right on my arm," Katie said. "All night."

"I hope I never have to eat through my veins," Pooch said. "It sounds horrible."

"It wasn't so bad," Katie said. "Everything else hurt so much, I didn't pay much attention to my arm."

She answered the rest of Pooch's questions then— well, most of them. She refused to discuss the bedpan with her little brother.

"I saved the newspapers for you," Mrs. Osborne said, as she put some papers on Katie's bed. "I knew you'd want to read the article about your accident and also the ones about the girl you know who's missing."

Katie picked up the top newspaper. There was a picture of Shannon on the front page.

"You know her?" Pooch said. "You know the girl who got kidnapped?"

"They aren't sure she was kidnapped," Mrs. Osborne said.

Katie started to read the article but Pooch kept asking so many questions that it was impossible to concentrate, so she finally put the paper down. She would read it later, after Pooch tired of talking and left her in peace.

She started to tell him and her mother how she'd met Shannon and how they'd liked each other right away. She just got to the part where Shannon asked her to go shopping, when the telephone rang and Mrs. Osborne left to answer it.

She came back almost immediately, a shocked look on her face.

"Linda's in labor," she said. "Mark's on his way home to take her to the hospital and I have to go get Sammy."

"But the baby isn't due for six more weeks," Katie said.

"I know," Mrs. Osborne said grimly. "Get your coat, Pooch. You're riding along."

"Do I have to?" Pooch said. "I want to stay and hear about how Katie's friend got kidnapped."

"You're coming with me," Mrs. Osborne said, in her don't-argue-with-me-just-do-as-I-say tone of voice. "Get your coat."

Reluctantly, Pooch left the room.

"I'm sorry to leave you here alone when you just got out of the hospital," Mrs. Osborne said.

"That's OK. I'll probably take another nap."

"I won't be gone more than an hour or so, just long enough to get over there, pack Sammy's things, and drive back here." She nudged Fred off the bed. "I'll put Fred out," she said, "so you don't have to worry about him if it takes me longer than I expect. Dad has to work late tonight."

Her mother talked fast, moving toward the door as she spoke. Katie could tell that she was plenty worried about Linda.

"Do you think the baby will be OK, Mom?" Katie asked. "How bad is it, to get born this much too early?"

"Anything can happen. We'll just have to wait and see." Mrs. Osborne whistled for Fred to follow her, and hurried out of the room.

Katie watched them go. Anything can happen. What did that mean? Might Linda's baby be born with something wrong with it? Maybe its arms would be missing or there would be something the matter with its heart. Katie felt sick to her stomach. She'd seen Sammy when he was only four days old and she couldn't believe how tiny he was. A baby who came six weeks early would be smaller still. Could it live? For the second time in as many days, Katie was afraid for someone else.

9

The note bothered Mr. Gates all day. Like a sliver under his skin, it irritated him. He couldn't get it completely out of his mind, even when he was lecturing his students about the Battle of Gettysburg.

There was something about it, something that didn't quite ring true, but he couldn't think what it was. Twice, between classes, he took the note out and read it again. Each time, as he put it away, he wondered what it was that disturbed him.

And then, long after the students had left for the day, just as Mr. Gates finished grading the last of the test papers on the Civil War, it came to him. He wasn't even thinking about the note when, inexplicably, he *knew*.

Mr. Gates put away his grade book, returned his empty coffee mug to the teacher's lounge, and left school for the day. Usually, he drove to his health club after school and spent an hour working out with the weights before he went home to dinner. That day, he made another stop first.

He'd never been to the Franklin Police Station before and he wasn't entirely sure he should be going there now. The police might not take his concern seriously at all.

It was just a short note, after all, from one student to another. He found them all the time. He never had figured out why students who complained bitterly when they were given a 200-word essay assignment would willingly write lengthy notes to each other, day after day. Especially the girls. The girls in his classes were forever getting into trouble for passing notes or reading notes or writing notes when they were supposed to be concentrating on their history lesson.

The police might glance at the note, decide he was the self-important busybody type, humor him a bit and then, as soon as he went on his way, toss the note in the wastebasket. He was sure they had to deal with strange people all the time and it would be easy to assume that a middle-aged schoolteacher with a note from one student to another, was just one more kook.

Except that Mr. Gates knew he wasn't a busybody, or

a person who tried to gain importance for himself by seeking to be a part of anything that smacked of notoriety. Mr. Gates was quite normal, thank you, and he had plenty to do with his time besides run to the police station with a piece of lined paper.

But he felt he had to go. In his spare time, Mr. Gates enjoyed detective novels and over the years he'd read hundreds of them. He was good at picking out the clues and he prided himself on correctly guessing the outcome of the books he read, even when the author intended the ending to be a surprise.

Perhaps it was all those years of looking for clues in books that alerted him. Something had made him read the note more than once and ponder its possible meaning. He wasn't sure if he'd found an important piece of evidence or not, but he wouldn't be able to live with himself if he didn't turn it in to the police.

He didn't know anything about the new girl, Katie Osborne. She seemed both pleasant and normal on the two days she was in his class, and if her parents cared enough about her schoolwork to call and arrange to pick up her assignments, chances are the kid was OK. In Mr. Gates's experience, students whose parents took an interest in their lives and encouraged them academically, usually didn't get into serious trouble.

Of course, there were exceptions to every rule and apparently Katie Osborne did go to Shannon Lindstrom's home on the very afternoon that Shannon disappeared. Maybe the friendly note was an attempt to cover something up.

There was always the chance that the police had not made all the facts in the case public. Maybe they were waiting for just such a piece of evidence to surface, so that they could make their move. Was this note the missing piece in Shannon's puzzling disappearance? Maybe. Maybe not.

He would let the police decide if it was important or not; that was their job.

He parked at the station, saw a desk marked "Information," and waited until the person behind the desk got off the phone.

"I'd like to speak to someone who's working on the Shannon Lindstrom case," he said.

"Your name, please?"

"John Gates. I'm a teacher at Franklin Middle School."

He had to wait only a few minutes before a police officer approached him. "Mr. Gates? I'm Lieutenant Collins. Let's step into this office, where we can talk."

As soon as they were seated, Mr. Gates explained why he was there. "One of my American History students is Katie Osborne," he said, "the girl who was in the hit-and-run accident. Katie's mother called the school and asked if the teachers could prepare some assignments for Katie to work on at home, while she's recuperating. Katie's books were in her locker so our principal opened the locker and had the books sent to the appropriate teachers, along with a memo explaining what was wanted."

He saw Lieutenant Collins shift restlessly in his chair so he reached in the inside pocket of his sports jacket and removed the folded piece of paper. He handed it to Lieutenant Collins.

"When I opened Katie's history book," Mr. Gates continued, "I found this note inside. As you can see, it's addressed to Shannon Lindstrom. Since Shannon is still missing, I thought I should read anything with her name on it. After I read it, I thought you should read it, too."

He waited then, while Lieutenant Collins unfolded the piece of paper and read the note.

"The part that bothers me," Mr. Gates said, when Lieutenant Collins looked up, "is where she asks if Shannon's brother told her that Katie was there."

Lieutenant Collins sat forward in his chair. He was frowning and listening carefully.

"According to what I read in the newspaper," Mr. Gates said, "Shannon's brother is only two years old. It doesn't seem likely that Katie would leave a message with a two-year-old child, or that a child so young would be home alone. If he wasn't alone—if someone else was there with him—Katie would have given the message to that person, not to the little boy."

"You're right," Lieutenant Collins said. "The Lindstrom boy is only two and he was at his regular day care center on Tuesday afternoon, as usual. His mother picked him up at 5:30, on her way home from work. Katie Osborne told me she went to the Lindstrom house about four o'clock."

"Then Katie spoke to someone else," Mr. Gates said. "Someone who pretended to be Shannon's brother." A little thrill of excitement shot through him. The note *was* important. It *was* a vital piece of evidence, just as he'd suspected.

Lieutenant Collins rose and extended his hand. "Thank you for bringing this in," he said, as the two men shook hands.

Mr. Gates got back in his car and headed toward his health club, to work out. He smiled with satisfaction as he drove. Who knows? The note might turn out to be the breakthrough in the Shannon Lindstrom case. He hoped so. It would please him no end to know that he personally helped to solve a crime.

As soon as Mr. Gates left, Lieutenant Collins reached for the telephone. He needed to talk to Katie Osborne again. Now.

The hospital receptionist answered but instead of

connecting him immediately to Katie Osborne's room, she put him on "Hold." Lieutenant Collins drummed his fingers impatiently on the desk. Finally the receptionist came back on the line.

"Katie Osborne was discharged this afternoon," she said. "She left more than an hour ago."

Lieutenant Collins hung up and immediately dialed the Osborne home. If they left the hospital an hour ago, they would easily be home by now.

The phone rang . . . and rang . . . and rang. Nine times. Ten times. He didn't understand it. Surely they would take the girl straight home and put her to bed. He must have misdialed. He hung up and immediately tried again, being careful to punch the proper numbers. There was still no answer.

Frustrated, he hung up and looked at the note again. This time, something else caught his attention and he dialed the number of the Lindstrom home.

Marcia Lindstrom, Shannon's mother, answered on the first ring.

"Have you found her?" she said, when Lieutenant Collins identified himself.

"Not yet," he replied, "but we have some new information. Did Shannon take a music lesson on Tuesday?"

"No," Mrs. Lindstrom said. "She's been wanting us to buy her a flute and let her start lessons but we haven't done it yet. Why?"

"One of her classmates thought Shannon was going to a piano lesson Tuesday."

"I can't imagine why anyone would think that. We don't even own a piano. Who was it? Who said that?"

"I can't tell you that yet. But we're pursuing the matter, you can count on that, and we'll call you the minute we know anything."

He dialed the Osbornes' number again but there was still no answer. They must have stopped somewhere on the way home from the hospital—to see a grandparent, perhaps, or have a hamburger. If it were *his* daughter, he'd take her home immediately but people did funny things. If twelve years of being a cop had taught him nothing else, it had surely taught him that.

He didn't let it ring so long this time. He had too much to do to sit there listening to the telephone ring. It was clear no one was home at the Osbornes'. On the fifth ring, he slammed the receiver down, put the note in Shannon Lindstrom's file, and went on to other matters.

He would have to talk to Katie Osborne later.

10

She heard the car start, back out of the driveway, and drive away. It was barely gone when the telephone rang. Katie debated. Should she try to get up out of bed and maneuver on her crutches into the living room to answer it? If it was Linda calling back, it wouldn't do any good; Mom was already on her way. Anybody else, Katie decided, would have to call back later. If she fell while she was here alone, she'd have Great Dane trouble and she had enough trouble already.

She leaned back and listened to the telephone ring— eight times, nine times, ten times before the caller finally hung up. She reached for the newspaper and the phone rang again.

This time she decided she should answer it. It must be important if whoever was calling would try again right away.

She threw back the covers and sat up. Her crutches were leaning against the headboard of the bed and she took one in each hand, got them under her arms, and stood up. It was the first time she'd tried to do it alone, without her mother or Pekinese there to hand her the crutches and steady her if she needed it.

She managed to get to her feet but she was slow. By the time she was ready to take her first step, the phone had already rung six times.

Hold on, she thought. *I'm coming as fast as I can.*

She was out the door of her room and starting down the hall when the ringing stopped. Katie stopped, too, completely exasperated. She wished whoever was trying to call would let it ring until she got there.

Clumsily, she turned around in the narrow hall and went back to her own room. She sat down on the bed, leaned the crutches against the headboard, and got her legs up on the bed. She was just pulling the covers up when the ringing started again.

This time she moved faster. She sat up, grabbed the crutches, stuffed them under her arms, and headed for the door, counting the rings. Two . . . three . . . four. She had already reached the living room. This time she would get there in time. Both times before, the caller held on for ten rings; she would easily get there before the tenth ring this time.

In the middle of the fifth ring, the sound suddenly stopped. The caller had hung up.

Katie said the worst word she could think of. Her mother would have an attack if she heard Katie say that but she couldn't help it. She was totally frustrated.

She decided not to get back in her own bed. Instead, she'd use her parents' bed, since there was an extension phone in their room. She wished she'd thought of that earlier.

She hobbled back to her own room first, to get the newspapers. She still wanted to read about Shannon and about her own accident. She tucked them under her chin and carried them that way.

By the time she got the bedspread folded back and got into her parents' bed, she was worn out but at least now she could reach the telephone. She lay still and waited for it to ring again. It didn't ring.

After a few minutes, she propped herself up against both pillows and started to read the article about Shannon that was on the front page of Wednesday's newspaper. Reading it brought back all her initial feelings of horror. The article said the same things that Mr. Gates had told her class that morning.

Shannon's face smiled at her from the newspaper and Katie studied the picture. It was a recent one; it looked just the way Shannon had looked on Tuesday when she waved good-bye at the corner.

Next she looked at Thursday's paper. Shannon's disappearance was still front page news. It said volunteers were searching all of the wooded areas surrounding Franklin, including the woods near Lake Duvall, but no sign of the missing girl had yet been found.

On the second page, there was a photograph of Shannon's family, holding a picture of Shannon. Katie looked at it. The people in the picture were identified as Marcia and Clyde Lindstrom and their son, Billy, age 2. Katie read it again, to be sure. That's what it said, all right. Age 2. And it wasn't a typographical error. The little boy in the photo was definitely about two years old.

She wondered if Shannon had two brothers, one ten years older and one ten years younger. It didn't seem likely. Katie looked at the photo again. Shannon's parents appeared to be much younger than her own parents. Shannon's mother didn't look much older than Linda.

Katie let the newspaper slip out of her hands. She thought back to her first day at school, when she and Shannon were walking together to second period class. How had Shannon said it? "There's ten years between my brother and me, too." Brother, singular. Not brothers, plural.

Because Linda was ten years older, Katie assumed Shannon's brother was ten years older, too. But Shannon never actually said that. And she had laughed when Katie said maybe Shannon would be an aunt before long, too. "No way," Shannon said.

Katie thought she meant *no way* because her brother wasn't married or *no way* because he didn't want kids but maybe she meant *no way* because her brother was only two years old and not about to become a father.

If that was true—if Shannon's brother was, indeed, only two, then who had answered the door when Katie knocked? Who was the young man who told her Shannon was taking her piano lesson?

She picked up the first article and quickly read it again. It said nothing about a piano lesson. It said only that Shannon apparently had come home from school because her purse was on the kitchen table, along with an apple with one bite missing. The Lindstrom house was locked and nothing of value was missing, which made police think that Shannon may have left willingly, perhaps with someone she knew.

If Shannon took a piano lesson after school, wouldn't it say so in the paper? Why didn't the reporter interview the piano teacher and verify what time Shannon left?

Because, Katie thought, there was no piano teacher to interview. Maybe there was no piano lesson. Maybe the man who answered the door that day didn't belong there at all. He hadn't wanted to answer; he only did so after she looked in the window and saw him standing there.

A shudder ran down Katie's back and she drew the covers up closer under her chin. She wished her mother hadn't had to leave.

She could hear Fred barking and she wondered if the neighbor's cat had climbed the fence into the Osbornes' yard again. About once a day since they moved in, Fluffy scaled the fence, prowled through the Osbornes' flower beds, and then got chased up the apple tree by Fred. Well, Fluffy would just have to stay in the tree tonight. Katie had enough problems without worrying about a cat.

Katie wondered what she should do. Should she wait until one of her parents got home and then tell them about the man she talked to that day? Or should she call the police right now?

The officer who came to the hospital to question her about the accident seemed nice and he knew about Shannon. Maybe she should call the police station and ask to talk to him. What was his name again? Lieutenant something. Collins. That was it. Lieutenant Collins. She didn't think he'd mind if she called him and told him what she was thinking. He wanted her to tell him everything she could remember about the accident and he believed her when she said the car swerved toward her. She was pretty sure he would want to know about this, too.

Fred's barking grew more frantic. It was the way he barked when the United Parcel Service man came to the door with a package and the way he used to bark at the garbage collectors every Thursday, back in Mill Valley. He must have Fluffy cornered under a shrub somewhere. Fred would be lucky if he didn't get his nose scratched and bloodied, the way he was carrying on.

She wished her dad would get home from work or that the neighbors would come over and rescue their own cat, for a change. It was too hard to think with all that racket, especially when she was so tired.

Abruptly, the barking stopped. Katie listened intently, wondering if Fluffy had somehow managed to scramble back up the fence to safety. If that happened, Fred would whine and howl at the fence for awhile, before giving up and returning to his doghouse.

She didn't hear Fred whine and howl. She didn't hear the barking start again, either. What she heard was the faint but unmistakable *click* of the back door closing.

Katie held her breath, waiting. Usually her dad came in the front door. The garage was still so full of boxes to be unpacked that he couldn't put his car in, so he parked on the street and used the front door. If it were him, he would holler, "Anybody home?"

He did that every night. If there was nobody there to greet him when he got home, he'd come in, pet Fred, hang his coat in the closet, and yell, "Anybody home?" And then her mom would call, "I'm in the kitchen," or "I'm in the bedroom," and if Katie and Pooch were home, they'd yell, too, and tell him where they were.

Dad knew she came home from the hospital today. He knew she'd be waiting to talk to him. If it was Dad in the kitchen, surely he would yell, "Anybody home?"

Nobody yelled.

Katie wanted to shout herself. She wanted to call out, "Is that you, Dad? I'm in here." But she didn't do it. If it was her dad, he'd find her soon enough. And if it wasn't him?

Katie's heart began to hammer. If it wasn't Dad, who was it? And how did he get in? Mom never went anywhere and left the house unlocked. She always reminded Katie to lock the doors, too. But Mom left in a terrible hurry, with her mind on Linda and the baby. Katie was sure Mom would have locked the front door when she went out, but what about the back door? In her rush to get to Linda's, was it possible that she forgot to lock it?

It was growing dark but Katie was glad she hadn't

yet turned on the light. At least it wasn't obvious which room she was in.

She strained her ears, trying to hear. Whoever it was, they were moving around in the kitchen. Katie swallowed. It must be a burglar and he was looking for something valuable to steal.

She lay still, hardly breathing. Maybe whoever it was would take the stereo and the TV and never come in the bedroom at all. She hoped so. She wouldn't even care if they took the brand new VCR, as long as they didn't come near her.

If it weren't for the cast on her leg, she might be able to climb out the window and go for help. As it was, she knew she could never get away in time. If the burglar found her . . . she didn't want to think about it.

She had barely escaped alive once this week already. She had no strength left to deal with this intruder.

And then it occurred to her that Mom may have called Dad from Linda's house, to tell him what was happening. She may have told him that Katie was home alone, taking a nap. That didn't explain why he would use the back door but it would explain why he didn't holler, "Anybody home?" the way he usually did. He might think she was asleep.

She had to find out who was in the house without giving away the fact that she was home, too. Slowly, she pushed the covers back and swung her legs over the side of the bed. She found her crutches, too, stood up, and started toward the window that looked out onto the street.

Let it be Dad, she thought, as she carefully made her way across her parents' bedroom in the dark. *Let me look out the window and see Dad's car parked in front, where he parks it every night.*

She had to move slowly, for fear of hitting something with one of her crutches and making a noise. It was so dark now that she could barely see.

She reached the window and looked out. There was a car parked in front of her house but it wasn't Dad's white Honda. It was an older car, with its front fender dented in. The streetlight was two houses down the block but even in the dim glow it shed, Katie could tell the car was green.

She stood still as a statue, staring out the window at it. And she knew, with a terrible certainty, that whomever was in the kitchen was not looking for something to steal.

He was looking for her.

11

Shannon landed in the gravel on the narrow shoulder of the road and immediately rolled into the shallow ditch. She lay still for an instant, wondering if any bones were broken. She didn't think so. She heard the car slow, stop, and start to turn around. Quickly, she scrambled to her feet and dashed for the grove of trees.

The underbrush made it hard to run, especially in a skirt. The brambles tore at her legs and reopened the wounds around her ankles, which had just begun to heal. She would reach the farmhouse sooner if she would use the lane, but she didn't dare.

David could drive down the lane much faster than she could run. She suspected he was already guilty of trying to kill Katie by running her down with his car;

what would prevent him from doing the same thing to her?

No, she had to stay in the woods, even though it was slower. If he came after her on foot, at least she had a head start.

Her foot caught in a vine and she tripped, falling to her knees and gashing her arm on the branch of a tree as she fell. Tears sprang to her eyes but she forced herself to get up and plunge onward. If she lay there feeling sorry for herself, he might find her. He was bigger, stronger—he could easily overtake her and then what would happen?

There was no outguessing him in his unbalanced state of mind. He might still think she was Angie and would punish her for running away from him. Or he might finally admit she wasn't Angie and then hate her for that. There was no point even trying to imagine his reaction. The important thing was not to get caught. She had to escape from him, permanently.

Her lungs ached from running so hard and there was a sharp crick in her side. She stopped running and leaned against a tree to catch her breath, straining her ears to hear if he was coming after her or not.

She heard the car. A moment later, through the trees, she caught a glimpse of it. He was driving slowly down the lane toward the farmhouse.

Shannon stayed on the far side of the tree trunk, where he couldn't see her. Her breath came a bit easier. If he was driving in the car, she was safe for the moment. She was afraid he would abandon the car and come after her, chasing her down in the woods like a hunter after a frightened doe.

The car went out of her sight but she stayed where she was, motionless, hiding behind the tree. Would he talk to the people at the house? Would he tell them lies about her, make it so they wouldn't believe her when she ran to them for help?

The car returned. It was going faster now, back up the lane toward the main road. Not enough time had elapsed for David to talk to anyone. He must have gone to the end of the lane, turned around, and come right back.

The car slowed suddenly and Shannon pressed tightly against the tree. Had he seen her?

He didn't stop but he continued to go slowly, not more than four or five miles per hour. Probably he was scanning the woods with his eyes, hoping to catch sight of her.

The car went out of her sight again and this time it did not return. She waited and listened for a long time, not daring to move. She was afraid he might have parked the car farther down the lane and come back on foot and she didn't want to give away her location. But she heard nothing more and saw nothing more.

She counted to a hundred, three different times, as a way of making herself wait longer. Then, when she still heard nothing, she cautiously left the protection of the tree trunk and started back toward the lane.

At the edge of the woods, she got down on all fours, even though it killed her knees to crawl on all those sticks and stones. She wanted to be able to look down the lane without being seen.

His car was gone. He had driven away and left her. She could hardly believe it. He must want to find Katie so much that he was willing to leave her behind, at least temporarily.

For three days, she had not been sure if she would live or die. She hadn't known if she would ever see her family again. She thought she might end her days tied up in an abandoned barn. Now, miraculously, she had escaped.

Now that she was finally free, all of her self-control departed. Tears of relief flowed down her cheeks and Shannon began to shake. All the fear and tension of the last three days seemed to seek release at the same time and her whole body trembled.

All she had to do now was get to the farmhouse, tell the occupants who she was, and wait for the police to come and get her. Or maybe her parents would be the ones to come. Was it possible that she was actually going to see her parents again?

She got to her feet, stepped out of the underbrush and onto the lane, and began walking toward the farmhouse. Every few seconds she glanced back over her shoulder, checking to be sure the green car wasn't coming. She saw nothing.

She wondered why he gave up so easily. When she jumped out of the car, he turned around immediately and came back to look for her. But he only drove down the lane and back once. Why didn't he try harder to find her?

There was only one explanation: his mind was still on Katie. The second he heard on the radio that Katie was going home from the hospital, his whole attitude changed. He became mean again, hard-looking, determined. When he looked at the piece of paper with Katie's name and address on it, his eyes were full of hatred.

Shannon started to run again. She had to tell someone. They had to send the police to Katie's house, to protect her, before David got there.

The yard around the farmhouse was unkempt. Once, long ago, there might have been lawns and flower beds surrounding it but now there were only weeds and tangled, tall grasses. An abandoned hay rake rusted beside an unsteady shed and cross-fencings of old barbed wire, in need of repair, outlined the side yard.

The house had once been white but there was little of the original paint left. Most of the boards, exposed to the weather, were now a mottled gray.

Bits of broken glass lay in mounds on the concrete porch steps. Gingerly, Shannon stepped over them and knocked on the door.

There was no answer. "Hello!" she called. "Is anybody here?"

Her voice seemed too loud and she looked anxiously around, wondering who could hear her.

This house gave her the shivers. It looked like something from a movie set, the kind of place a director would choose for a ghost story or a murder mystery. It certainly was not the haven she'd hoped to find at the end of the lane, with friendly, sympathetic people ready to help her.

She pounded on the door again. "Hello, in there," she cried. "I need help!"

The sun was starting to set and the woods looked dark now, and threatening. Shannon left the porch and went around to the back side of the house. There was no sign of life. She pounded furiously on the back door, imploring someone to come, but no one did.

Her fists hurt from hammering on the wooden door. She knew it was useless but she was unable to stop. She didn't know where else to go for help. This was the only driveway she remembered seeing for miles. She couldn't go out to the road and try to walk to town. David might come back and he'd see her for sure.

No, she thought. He wasn't coming back. He was going after Katie. She had to get help for Katie before David got there.

She quit pounding on the door and tried the door knob. If there was no one to let her in, she'd have to let herself in.

The door was locked. She removed her shoe, lifted it over her head, and whacked at the glass windowpane in the back door. It shattered, sending a sprinkling of glass into the house. Shannon reached through the hole, scratching her arm badly on the jagged edge, and opened the door from the inside.

It was even darker inside the house. She felt on the wall for a light switch but when she clicked it on, nothing happened.

The house smelled moldy and stale, as if there had been no fresh air in it for many months. As her eyes grew accustomed to the dim light, she could see a few pieces of furniture—a table and three chrome chairs, an overstuffed chair with the coiled springs sticking up out of the seat cushion, a rickety-looking coffee table heaped with old papers.

She had to find the telephone. That's all that mattered now. The house could be filled with priceless antiques and they wouldn't interest her. All she wanted was to find a telephone and call for help.

She walked through an archway from the kitchen toward the main room and then jumped back again, brushing frantically at her eyes. A cobweb clung to her cheek and dangled from her chin.

Shannon glanced quickly at all the places where a telephone might logically be. She saw nothing. Either it had been disconnected and taken away, or else there never was one. She had counted on telephoning for help but it wasn't going to happen.

Wearily, she sat down on one of the chrome chairs and put her head in her hands. Now what?

It was tempting to stay here in the old house for the night. Now that she was inside, she knew no one lived here anymore. It wasn't as cold inside as the barn had been and there was an old, worn sofa that she could sleep on. Briefly, she considered how good it would feel to lie down and let the exhaustion she felt give way to sleep. Then—in the morning, when it was light and she could see where she was going—she could find help.

Except the morning would be too late for Katie. She knew that. It might already be too late for Katie but she couldn't give up, not while there was still a chance that she could reach help in time to prevent another tragedy.

She would have given anything for a peanut butter sandwich and a cold glass of milk. Especially the milk. She'd been thirsty ever since David tied her up, because the sweet orange soda never quenched her thirst. Now, especially after running so hard in the woods, her mouth felt like it was filled with sponges.

She returned to the kitchen and turned on the faucet. A series of gurgles and gasps came out, followed by a trickle of water. Even in the faint light, it had a definite brownish tinge to it. Shannon waited a few seconds until the brown color got fainter and then almost disappeared.

She scooped some of the water into her hands and splashed it on her face. It felt wonderful. She filled her hands again and sniffed at it. It had a mineral-like odor but it wasn't too strong and it didn't smell stagnant. She decided to take a chance. She drank two handfuls of the cold water; she had never tasted anything more delicious in her life.

The water refreshed her and renewed her determination. Much as she might like to lie down and sleep, she knew she could not stay. She would have to walk back down the lane and then walk along the road toward town. They had passed a man on a bicycle this afternoon; surely there would be *some* traffic on the road at night. She would flag down the first car that came along and have them drive her into town. If the first car turned out to be David, coming back to look for her—well, she just had to take a chance on that.

Shannon wiped her wet, dirty hands on her already-filthy skirt and went out the way she'd come in.

The lane seemed longer going back than it had when she came in, maybe because when she was approaching the house, she had hope that her ordeal was nearly over. Now, she wasn't so sure. Her legs ached and her shoulder throbbed where she'd landed on it when she jumped out of David's car. She was weak, both from hunger and fear. Could she make it if she had to walk all the way into town? She didn't know. But she knew she had to try. She was the only person in the whole world who knew that David was after Katie. She had to hurry. She had to get help.

As she neared the end of the lane, she heard a car approaching. She began to run and she reached the end of the lane, by the mailbox, just as a pair of headlights came into sight, heading toward town.

Shannon waved her arms frantically and ran toward the car. It was a big station wagon, the kind with wood paneling on the sides. It slowed as she approached it.

"Stop!" Shannon yelled. "Please stop!"

The car rolled past her and slowed to a stop. Shannon turned and ran after it.

"Please!" she cried. "I need a ride into town."

She couldn't see the driver of the car. She wasn't close

enough yet and the taillights glared in her eyes. But she heard the voice. It was a woman's voice and the woman sounded angry.

"Shame on you," the woman said. "Hitching a ride at your age. Don't you realize you could be picked up by some—some murderer?"

"But you don't understand," Shannon said. She had reached the back fender of the station wagon and she put out her hand to steady herself.

"You go back home immediately," the woman said. "And don't you ever hitchhike again!"

"Wait!" Shannon cried. "I need help!" But even as she said the words, she felt the station wagon move out from under her hand. "Come back!" she screamed. And then she stood, trembling, in the dark at the side of the road, watching the red taillights disappear toward town.

She trudged blearily after them. She was too tired to run anymore, too tired even to walk very fast. She kept her head down and plodded onward, one foot after the next. It was the best she could do.

She came to the old school but she knew there was no point trying to go inside it. If the farmhouse lacked a telephone, the school would, too. She walked on, wondering if it was already too late to help Katie.

And then she heard it. The loud, powerful sound of a truck engine. She lifted her head and saw the bright lights coming straight toward her. It was a large truck, the kind with a separate cab. At least she knew it wasn't David, returning to hunt for her.

Once more, Shannon stepped out into the road and waved her arms. The truck slowed immediately and wheezed to a stop.

"I need help," Shannon called as she ran toward it.

Instantly, the driver stopped the engine, got out of his truck, and ran toward her.

"I'm Shannon Lindstrom," she cried. "I was kidnapped and I got away from him and I have to get to town."

"My God," the man said. "You're the kid who's missing. I saw your picture on the TV last night." His strong arm went around her for support and he half-carried her the rest of the way to his truck. He helped her into the cab and then climbed in beside her.

"Are you OK?" he asked.

He was about her father's age, with a scruffy beard. He had on a plaid wool shirt and a cap that said, "Keep on Truckin'." Shannon thought he was the most beautiful human being she'd ever seen.

"I'll be all right," she said. "But we have to get into Franklin. We have to call the police and tell them he's after Katie."

"Who is?"

"His name is David and he thinks I'm his sister, only

I'm not, and he tied me up in a barn and now he's going to kill Katie because she saw him at my house. He already tried to once and now he's going back again and nobody knows he's after her except me and we have to stop him."

Shannon knew she was babbling. Her words ran together and she was crying at the same time and she wasn't sure any of it made sense but she couldn't help herself.

"Take it easy, kid," the man said. "We'll call for help. You just take it easy, now."

He reached forward and picked up a microphone. Shannon watched as he pushed a button and began to talk.

"Break nine. Break nine. This is KCB136 and I got an emergency here. Are there any Smokies listening?"

The answer crackled back on the CB radio immediately. "Go ahead, breaker. We're listening."

"This is Fuzzy Bear. I just picked up the kid who's been missing."

"Shannon Lindstrom?"

"Yeah. Shannon."

"What's your 10-20?"

"About fifteen miles east of Franklin, on Old Highway 3."

"10-4. What's Shannon's condition?"

"She's OK but she says the guy who took her is after another kid. Katie . . ." He paused, looked at Shannon questioningly, and then handed her the mike.

"Katie Osborne," Shannon said. She tried to speak slowly and clearly, but it wasn't easy when she was so excited. "She lives somewhere near me but I'm not sure where. He tried to kill her once before, two days ago, by running her down with his car and . . ."

"10-4," the voice said. "Stand by." There was a long pause. Shannon wasn't sure what to do. She looked at the truck driver. Fuzzy Bear. It was a good name for him. He put his finger to his lips and winked at her and she knew to be quiet and wait. In a moment, the voice came back on the radio. "We have Katie Osborne's address," it said. "Two units are on the way there."

"Hurry!" Shannon cried. "He has a big knife and he's crazy. Really crazy."

"Do you know his name?" the voice asked.

"David. That's all I know. Just David. He thought I was his sister. He kept calling me Angie."

"10-4. What about a description? What does he look like?"

"He's tall," Shannon said, "and he has reddish hair and there's a scar on his face."

"Age?"

"About 20. Or 22."

"10-4. Stand by."

There was another, longer pause. Then the voice said, "David Dempsey. Ex-mental patient. Released from State Hospital to a halfway house two weeks ago. Reported missing from the halfway house. Five feet eleven inches, 180 pounds, scar on forehead."

"That's him!" Shannon said. "And he has an old green car. License number . . ." She thought carefully. Pigs Eat Slop and Billy's birthday. "License number PES-211."

"Way to go, kid," said Fuzzy Bear. He reached for the microphone and spoke into it. "This is Fuzzy Bear again. Where do you want me to take her?"

"I want to go home," Shannon said.

"Take her home," the voice said. "We'll notify her parents that you're on the way and we'll have a doctor and one of our units waiting."

"10-4," said Fuzzy Bear. "This is KCB136. Over and out." He replaced the microphone and started the engine. "You're goin' home, kid," he said.

Shannon smiled. For the first time since last Tuesday, when David surprised her in the kitchen, she smiled.

The tired feeling was gone, replaced by excited anticipation. Her shoulder still hurt and her ankles were sore and she knew she was covered with cuts and scratches and her hair was a total mess and she hadn't had a shower or a change of clothes for three days but she didn't care. She was going home. That's all that mattered. She was going home.

She leaned her head against the back of the seat. She hoped the call had been in time to help Katie. She wasn't sure how long ago David drove away, and left her hiding in the grove of trees. Had he already done whatever he planned to do? Or would the police reach Katie's house in time?

12

Why?

The word pounded in Katie's brain as she stood at the window, looking out at the car. Why did someone want to kill her? Why had he tried to run her down with his car? It *wasn't* an accident; she knew that now. But why? What had she done?

There were no answers; only questions. She had to think. There was no way she could climb out a window and go for help. Not with a cast on her leg. Help would have to come to her.

The telephone. Of course. She would quietly use the telephone. She couldn't see to dial in the dark but she could dial 0 and ask an Operator to send someone to help her.

Cautiously, trying not to make any sound, she moved back from the window, to the foot of her parents' bed. From there, she could see down the hallway. The light was still on in the kitchen but she didn't hear anything.

The telephone was on a small nightstand beside the bed. There wasn't room for her to get between the bed and the wall, not on crutches. She would have to go back to the other side of the bed, get on the bed, and roll over to the side where the telephone was.

She turned around, went back to the side of the bed that faced the window, and sat down. She leaned her crutches against the headboard. She managed to get both feet on the bed again, by lifting the cast with her hands, and then she quickly rolled toward the wall, reaching for the telephone.

Her heart was beating so hard, it seemed to her it could be heard clear in the kitchen. Her hand groped for the receiver.

One of the crutches clattered to the floor. Katie tensed, terror-stricken, before she realized what it was. In her haste, she had not made sure the crutches were secure and now her movement on the mattress had dislodged one.

She heard footsteps coming down the hall. Her fingers felt frantically in the dark for the last button on the phone and she pushed it as hard as she could. She heard it ring. Once. Twice. The footsteps came closer.

They turned into Katie's bedroom. Did he just go into the first room he came to? Or did he know which room was hers?

She pulled the covers up over her head, pressing the receiver to her ear.

Three rings. Four.

"Operator. May I help you?"

Katie whispered. "I need help."

"Hello? This is the Operator."

"I need help," Katie said again, louder this time.

"What's your address?"

"Six Crestwood Drive. No. That's wrong. I mean . . ." Katie stopped. Six Crestwood Drive was their house in Mill Valley. This house was . . . but she couldn't talk anymore. She could hear him coming. He'd left her bedroom and was coming toward her, into her parents' bedroom.

Katie held the telephone hard against the mattress, so he wouldn't hear the Operator's voice. They would trace the call. She had watched TV enough to know that. As long as Katie didn't hang up the phone, they could trace the call and get her address and send help.

But how long did that take? Could anyone get here in time?

There was no overhead light in her parents' room, only two lamps on the bedside tables. She could hear him fumbling in the dark, cursing under his breath.

She heard the lamp click on and, even with the covers over her head, she could tell the room was light now.

The covers were pulled away and Katie looked up at him. It was Shannon's brother. Only she knew now that he wasn't Shannon's brother at all.

"What do you want?" she said, trying not to sound too scared. Maybe she could keep him talking until help arrived.

He didn't answer. There was a strange, savage look in his eyes. Like a dog with rabies, Katie thought. He's a golden retriever gone mad.

There was a knife in his hand, a big one, the kind the Osbornes always used to chop vegetables or cut a sandwich in two. Katie began to tremble.

Fred started barking again, the frantic, loud bark that he always used when a stranger came into his yard. She knew now he hadn't been barking at Fluffy before; he'd been barking at this man. But why was he barking now? Were there two men?

The man looked down at her. "I can't let you tell," he said. "If you tell, they'll lock me up again. They'll keep Angie away from me and they'll lock me up and that's why I have to do this. I can't let you tell!"

He raised the knife.

"Wait!" Katie cried. "I won't tell anyone! I promise!"

The man hesitated.

"I swear I haven't told anyone about you," Katie said. "And I won't. Please! You have to believe me."

She could see the confusion in his eyes. She knew he was wondering if he could believe her. She had to convince him. It was her only hope.

"I thought you were Shannon's brother," she said, "and so I never . . ."

She didn't finish the sentence. She heard a siren, nearby, and she stopped talking, wondering if help had arrived. She knew the man heard it, too, for he stood still, listening.

The room was suddenly flooded with blue light. It whirled quickly around the walls, like a strobe light. Katie realized it must be shining from the top of a police car.

The man's hand was stopped in midair and the blue light glinted off the blade of the knife. He looked behind him, at the window, where the light was coming from.

Katie lay still, knowing instinctively that she should not call his attention back to her.

The man lowered his knife and walked slowly toward the window until he was close enough to look out. Katie saw his whole body tense. Then he turned around and came back to her bedside.

"You told," he said, and he raised the knife again. There was raw hatred in his eyes as he loomed over her.

"You told the police."

13

The truck rumbled noisily through the quiet residential streets. If Shannon hadn't been so tired, and so worried about Katie, she would have enjoyed the stares of the people they passed.

The seat she sat on was so high that she looked down on the tops of the cars they passed.

"Turn right at the next corner," she said. She sat forward on the edge of her seat. She was almost home.

They rounded the corner and saw the flashing blue lights of two police cars. The street was blockaded.

"Wait here," Fuzzy Bear said. "I'll tell them who you are."

He jumped out of the cab and strode quickly to one

of the police officers. Immediately, the officer came over to talk to Shannon.

"The whole neighborhood's closed to traffic," he said. "We think David Dempsey's in the Osborne house and Katie may be in there with him. Alone."

"Alone!" boomed Fuzzy Bear.

"We're trying to talk him into coming out," the officer said.

"I can help," Shannon said. "I think I can get him to come out."

The police officer looked skeptical. "The guy's looney," he said. "He was in the State Hospital for years and now he's apparently had a relapse. We'll handle him; you stay here, where it's safe."

"NO!" Shannon cried. The officer looked surprised. She was surprised herself. Under ordinary circumstances, Shannon wouldn't dream of talking back to a police officer. But these were not ordinary circumstances. Katie needed help.

"I know he's crazy," Shannon said. "But I think he'll listen to me. He told me things, things about himself. I think he'd come out if I could talk to him."

"A doctor from the State Hospital is already talking to him," the officer said.

"She *did* spend the last three days with him," Fuzzy Bear said. "And she's a smart kid; she remembered the license number."

The officer looked hard at Shannon. "Maybe you should talk to the doctor," he said. He took her hand and started to run down the street.

"I'm going with her," Fuzzy Bear said, as he grabbed Shannon's other hand.

To her relief, the officer didn't object.

The brick house was lit up like it was high noon in July. Police cars were parked everywhere and as she approached, Shannon could hear a voice on a loudspeaker, urging David to surrender.

She saw the green car parked by the curb. Two officers were examining the front fender. She heard an exclamation as one of the officers realized who she was.

"It's her. It's the Lindstrom girl."

The officer she was with motioned to the doctor and the loudspeaker ceased. Quickly, the officer explained who Shannon was and the doctor asked a few questions about what David had said and done while he was with Shannon.

The police and the doctor conferred briefly and then the doctor handed the microphone to Shannon.

"You have one minute to talk to him," the officer said. "After that, we're going in after him."

Her knees were shaking as she took the microphone in her hands. If Fuzzy Bear hadn't put his arm around her, to support her, she might not have been able to stand.

Inside the house, Katie lay terrified, staring at the point of the knife as it came closer to her throat.

"David!" Shannon called. "It's me, Angie. I've come back for you and we're going to go away together, just the two of us." The buzz of voices and the movement of people near the Osborne house ceased. All eyes were on Shannon. "Don't hurt Katie," she pleaded. "If you hurt Katie, they'll lock you up again. If you come out of the house now, we can go away and live on our little farm." Shannon started to cry. "Can you hear me, David? It's Angie! Angie is waiting for you to come out."

The tears streamed down Shannon's face and she couldn't continue. Silently, the officer took the microphone from her hand. No one spoke. They waited, watching the Osbornes' house.

The seconds ticked by and there was no sound from inside the house.

"We're going to have to go in after him," an officer said. "Alert the units in back that we're . . ."

He stopped. The front door of the house had opened. David stepped outside and stood alone, blinking into the bright lights and shielding his eyes with his hand.

"Angie?" he said. "Where are you?"

Instantly, two police officers overwhelmed him. The knife fell to the ground and handcuffs were snapped on David's wrists. He didn't struggle.

A frantic-looking man in a business suit dashed from the next yard toward the front door of the house. "Katie?" he yelled. "Are you all right?"

One of the officers stopped him. "Let us go in first, Mr. Osborne," he said. "We don't know what we'll find."

Shannon watched as David was led away from the house, toward one of the waiting patrol cars. Before David got in, he stopped and looked up. He was only a few feet from Shannon and he looked directly at her.

Shannon tensed. She felt Fuzzy Bear's arm tighten around her.

She thought David would hate her for lying to him but his eyes, when he looked at her, held no emotion. The wildness was gone. There was no hatred, no regret, no sadness. They were blank, empty. When he looked at her, he looked straight through her, as if he didn't see her at all. Then he turned and climbed into the police car.

Shannon knew she had every reason to despise this man but she no longer felt any hatred. She felt only pity and a terrible sadness because she was quite sure he would now be locked up for the rest of his life.

At that moment, Shannon realized that her intention of becoming a psychiatrist had never been serious before. She'd used it as an attention-getter, a way to make her parents take her seriously. Even last summer when she read parts of *The Psychology of the Insane,* it had been more for the shock value of carrying the book around than out of sincere interest in the subject matter.

But now she was interested. She knew now that mental patients are not just "crazies." They are real people—people who love their sisters, and mourn their dead mothers, and yearn for a better future.

As she watched David ride away in the patrol car, Shannon made a commitment to herself. When the time came, she would apply for medical school. Maybe someday, when she was a psychiatrist, she would have a patient like David. If she did, she hoped she'd be able to help him.

14

"There's going to be a special assembly for us," Shannon said. "As soon as you can come back to school."

It was Monday, Shannon's first day back at school, and she'd come straight to Katie's house when school got out.

"No kidding!" Katie said, as she took some more popcorn. She was sitting on top of her bed with her leg propped up on a pillow and Fred stretched out beside her.

"It was unreal at school today," Shannon said. "Everybody wanted to talk to me. I mean, *everybody*. I felt like I was a movie star or something."

"Well, you did save my life. You deserve to be treated like a celebrity."

"Wasn't that picture of us in the newspaper terrible? You with your cheek all scratched up and wearing your pajamas and me with my clothes a mess and my hair looking like a Frankenstein wig."

"We made quite a pair, all right," Katie said. "You look much better today."

"So do you."

"I feel better, too, now that David Dempsey is back in the State Hospital."

"Lieutenant Collins came to my house yesterday," Shannon said. "He told us that David had severe psychological problems as a child. Then, when he was fourteen, a drunk driver smashed into the car he was riding in and his mother and his sister were both killed. He had a complete mental breakdown a few weeks later and had to be committed to the mental hospital. He was released to a halfway house two weeks ago and was getting along fine. He had a part-time job as a dishwasher and he was learning to drive and then, just by a quirk, he happened to see a car accident where a woman was seriously hurt. Apparently, it made him remember when his mother and Angie were killed. He had a complete relapse, just like that, and he was right back to how he was after the accident, all those years ago. He decided he'd go home and find his sister, like he wanted to do then."

"And he thought you were his sister."

"That's right. David used to live in my house. After his mother and sister died, the house was sold to the people we bought it from. Only, David didn't know that. He found his old house, let himself in, and then, when he saw me, he thought I was Angie."

"It gives me the creeps to think about it," Katie said. "Whose car did he have? Did he steal it?"

"It belonged to one of the workers at the halfway house." Shannon looked thoughtful. "Think of all the people who've been hurt because of that one drunk driver," she said.

"I know one thing," Katie said. "When I'm old enough to drive, the only thing I'll drink is orange soda."

"Not orange soda!" Shannon cried. "Yuck!"

Before she could explain, Mrs. Osborne knocked on Katie's bedroom door. "You have more company," she said.

It was Brooke and Pam, the Pomeranian and the Doberman. Katie hadn't expected to see them.

"We saw you on the news Friday night," Pam said. "We brought you some cookies."

"Thanks," Katie said. "How did the awards banquet go the other night?"

"It was great!" Pam said.

"Pam won Player of the Year," Brooke said.

"Congratulations!" Katie and Shannon spoke together and then laughed.

"You guys should try out for basketball next year," Pam said.

"Me?" Shannon said. "El Shrimpo?"

"You're tall, like me," Pam said to Katie. "I'll bet you'd be good at basketball."

"You guys are so lucky," Brooke said. "I'd give anything to be tall."

Lucky? Katie thought. Being tall is lucky?

"I used to pray I'd get a growth spurt," Shannon said, "But now I've given up."

"I used to pray I'd *quit* growing," Katie said.

"Too bad you can't cut off a couple of inches and give them to me."

"And me," Brooke said.

"After you get the cast off your leg," Pam said, "maybe you could come over to my house some time and shoot baskets. I need to keep in practice."

"Sure," Katie said. "That would be fun."

"Hey!" Brooke said. "Can I sign your cast?"

"Me first," Shannon said. "Katie already told me I got to sign it first."

Katie pointed to the colored markers and the girls took turns signing their names on her cast. As Katie watched them, she threw back her shoulders and sat up straight, the way her mother was always telling her to do. There wasn't much point in scrunching all the time if the kids here in Franklin liked her tall.

Pooch came charging into the room. "I gave a speech about you at school today," he announced. "I told all about how you almost got murdered and how the police were here and how the kidnapper got arrested right on our front walk."

Katie was tempted to point out that Pooch had not been home when any of this happened but she restrained herself. He had been so furious when he found out that he missed all the excitement while he and Mrs. Osborne were over at Linda's, getting Sammy, that Katie didn't have the heart to mention it now. Instead, she introduced her brother while he helped himself to the popcorn and fed two kernels to Fred. Pooch, she thought, was aptly named. He was like a puppy—all wiggly and excitable, with a tendency to bark at all the wrong times, but lovable, all the same.

Pooch, she knew, wouldn't want her to think of him as a puppy. She wondered how Brooke and Pam would feel if they knew she thought of them as the Pomeranian and the Doberman.

And Shannon? What kind of dog did Shannon remind her of? Shannon was short and happy, like a dachshund. She was smart, like a poodle. But she had a narrow, pretty face and reddish blonde hair. A collie? No, that wasn't quite right, either.

Maybe, she decided, Shannon was that most wonderful of all dogs, a mutt. A mixed breed. That's what the

Osbornes' veterinarian called Fred—a mixed breed.

Once, while Katie was waiting in the vet's office for Fred to have his rabies vaccination, she read an article about mixed breeds. The author said certain mixed breed dogs make the best companions because they're so loyal and friendly. He even suggested that the American Kennel Club should have a new official category for them, called Companion Dogs.

"If dogs in general are considered man's best friend," the article stated, "then Companion Dogs surely should be honored as our true friends."

Katie wondered if that's what Shannon would become. Her true friend.

Brooke and Pam were talking about a boy in their algebra class. "What a brain," Brooke said. "He could teach the class, if they'd let him."

"That reminds me," Shannon said. "My folks gave me a welcome home present yesterday."

"What did you get?" Brooke asked. "A new outfit?"

Shannon shook her head.

"What then?" Pam said. "Some albums?"

"They gave me a life-size model of the human brain. It shows all the different parts and has them all labeled and there's a book with it that tells how each part works."

Katie could tell that Brooke and Pam were not thrilled over Shannon's gift but she thought it was wonderful.

She knew it meant that Shannon's parents had decided their daughter wasn't a baby, after all.

That thought reminded her of *her* big news. In all the commotion, she almost forgot it.

"I'm an aunt again," she said. "My sister had a baby girl Saturday."

"Already?" Shannon said.

"She only weighs five pounds but she's healthy. And guess what? Linda and Mark named her Jennifer Shannon. In your honor."

"That's great," Shannon said. "I guess that makes me an honorary aunt."

"If it was a boy, they probably would have named him after me," Pooch said. He handed Shannon a three-ring binder. "Would you sign your name in my notebook?" he asked.

"Sure," Shannon said. She opened the binder and wrote her name on the first page.

"More than once," Pooch said. "Maybe you could sign twenty or thirty pages."

"Pooch . . ." Katie said.

"What for?" Shannon said.

"I'm going to sell your autograph at school tomorrow," Pooch said. "I bet I can get at least a quarter each for them and if you do twenty, that's . . ."

"Out," Katie said, pointing to the door.

"But I want to stay and . . ."

"Out!"

"Pooch," Mrs. Osborne called. "Come out here. Katie's talking with her friends now. You can see her later."

Pooch took his notebook and left, grumbling to himself.

Katie's talking with her friends. Katie liked the way that sounded. She reached for a cookie, looked at Shannon, and smiled.

PEG KEHRET earned her first by-line at the age of eight when she wrote, hand-printed, and distributed a newspaper about the dogs in her neighborhood. As an adult she's published more than 250 short stories and articles in national magazines and her award-winning plays have been produced in all fifty states. Her book, *Winning Monologs for Young Actors,* has helped countless would-be thespians get their first roles.

Peg lives with her husband and an assortment of pets in an eighty-year-old farmhouse near Seattle, Washington. She is a long-time volunteer at The Humane Society & SPCA, a frequent workshop leader for the Pacific Northwest Writer's Conference, and a fiction instructor for Writer's Digest School.

TILLAMOOK COUNTY LIBRARY
210 Ivy
Tillamook, Oregon
842-4792

1. Borrowers are responsible for books drawn on their card.
2. Fine-5¢ a day for overdue books.
3. Scotch tape use, other injury to books and losses must be made good to Library's satisfaction.